The Thunder
of What You Are

by

Parfait LaRouche

DORRANCE
PUBLISHING CO
EST. 1920
PITTSBURGH, PENNSYLVANIA 15238

Dorrance Publishing Co
585 Alpha Drive
Suite 103
Pittsburgh, PA 15238
Visit our website at *www.dorrancebookstore.com*

ISBN: 978-1-4809-5812-8
eISBN: 978-1-4809-5835-7

Thank you to all of my family and friends near and far for your constant encouragement and support. I am forever indebted to you all for helping me realize my vision.

To all my girls who suffer with mental health issues in silence, there is help, seek it, embrace it, and become the best version of you.

※

Zee

Black women aren't allowed to be depressed.

We are burdened with the motto "Strong Black Women," which seldom allows us to ever be weak.

We can't get too loud, or state our opinion too aggressively, for fear of being labeled an angry black woman.

So here we are, trapped in our truth, crippling under the pressure of our expectations, tied to the yolk of strength beyond measure, we can't unload our secrets, except to one another, and even then, we are cautious, treading lightly, never stepping too hard, never planting our foot into our existence.

※

I wrote that poem ten years ago, when I was a naive sophomore at the prestigious HBCU, Florida A&M University, the beacon on the top of seven hills. I could not have been more excited to be attending the same institution as my high school mentors, the infamous "set" where so many first met and fell in love. While many of my friends opted for Bethune Cookman College, Spelman, or Florida Atlantic University, I always knew I would be a Rattler, home of an internationally known famous band, a world-class business school and top-notch engineering program. I treasured the intricate communities that held the stories of generations. I basked in the southern hospitality and secretly named my beloved school "The Pride of the South," although it was located in the uppermost northern part of Florida, in Tallahassee. Those four years were the best years of my life, filled with lifelong friends, sorority sisters, and the best professors on planet earth. There was Dr. Harrison, my psychology professor, who loved to engage students with humor while still leaving us yearning to become part of the next social movement to revolutionize mental healthcare. I can still remember being in his class and laughing so hard at his jokes, but still appreciating the seriousness of his subject matter. There was Dr. Jones, who could solve any mathematical problem and challenged his students to do the same, all while instilling in us a love for all things number related. He made me shed the narrative that I was given that I would always just be mediocre at math and helped me to become a stellar student. There was my admissions counselor, resident assistant, and cafeteria worker, drank. I drank and I drank some more, irresponsibly. After about three hours, I was ready to head back to the dorm, but of course no one else was, and I didn't blame them. Why should they end their night because I couldn't handle my liquor? The night was still young, and many of my friends had plans to head over to the Steak and Shake, a 24-hour restaurant, to have a fun-filled nightcap, but my stomach and my head had other plans. The music was blaring, playing the latest and greatest hits of hip-hop, R&B and dancehall reggae. The beat of every drum was pulsating throughout my entire body. I could feel the room spinning. I kept going back and forth to the bathroom, my stomach tied in knots, my mouth filled with saliva. The spit, like a waterfall, cascading down my mouth, into the toilet, some remnants remained on my chin. And then I saw him, the guy I said hello to every morning when we crossed paths on my way to the School of Business building. His glare was always welcoming and reassuring. The guy who occasionally sat at the same table with me at the on-campus café, and like clockwork always placed the same order: cheeseburger, French fries and the sweet tea special, the guy I danced with on the "set" nonchalantly on those Fridays, when everyone skipped the class they had registered for, and opted for the lessons learned on the most popular spot on the yard. The guy who shared an umbrella with me on that rainy day, when we both got caught up in one of those infamous Tallahassee rainstorms that lasted for less than ten minutes. That guy. I knew him, even though our interactions never lasted longer than maybe ten to fifteen minutes, I knew him. I bumped into him on my way out of the bathroom for the umpteenth time. He shared with me that he was ready to leave too, and offered me a ride back to my side of campus. BINGO! I felt as if I had hit the lottery. I would get to go home and sleep off this enormous headache and nausea. In his car, we listened to music, and tripped on how fast the year was going by. He made a turn that I didn't recognize, but I thought maybe he knew a shortcut. I knew him. He stopped in a secluded place, under the nighttime skyline, the trees resembled ghosts decked in green leaves, the branches' mimicking arms looking to wrap me up in its foundation. Before I could try to get my bearings together and reach out to the trees for their warmth, I could feel the dry stubble of his freshly shaven face rub against my cheek. He leaned over to kiss me, his mouth wet, and his breath reeked of alcohol and peppermints, as if each represented two sides of him. A weird combination. It is funny what the mind remembers. The trees, and the rag in the back seat. Why didn't I notice the rag in the back seat when I first got into the car? Why didn't I question my whereabouts as soon as he made a turn on the road less traveled? Why didn't I pay more attention during know, there was no escaping the inevitable. My eyes burned, and my lips quivered, I could taste the blood in my mouth, my jaw throbbed, but I knew better to resist any more. I thought to myself if I lay still, it would be over soon, and just like that it was. I could not find my voice; it had left me momentarily.

Afterward, he drove me home. We rode in complete silence. The only noise was the occasional car horn and tires screeching down a long lonely road. The ride seemed to take forever, but in all actuality, it was maybe fifteen minutes. When he stopped the car, I methodically made my way out, not wanting to make eye contact with him. I just wanted to resign to something familiar. Usually when I arrived at my dorm, I was always willing to share my late-night escapades with the Resident Assistant, but not tonight; I could only afford to give her eye recognition and a head nod. I hurried to my suite, which I shared with three other roommates. The steps seemed unbearable, as if every step was a labor in defiance. I immediately jumped into the shower and tried to wash the memory of the night away. Afterward, I lay down, still gasping for air, replaying the night's events over and over again in my head. I thought about going to the campus police and then thought, and say what? Not to mention, I had just washed away any DNA evidence there was on me. There was also the fact that he could say it was consensual. I imagined every possible scenario in my head. I tried looking for the trees in my thoughts, hoping maybe the image of them would force me to confront my reality and advocate for myself. What would my story be? The truth was this guy I barely knew took my inebriated self from a party, where I agreed to ride with him, and he raped me. The truth was: Who am I? Who would believe this black girl? The only strength I had left in me was to write this poem. It served as my confession, as the statement I couldn't bring myself to make. I always regretted it. Maybe my voice could have helped someone else on or off campus. Maybe he needed to be held accountable so that no one else would experience the depth of pain that I did. But I wasn't strong enough for myself, let alone others. After that day, I encountered him several more times on campus, at parties, in the café, or on the "set." Every time I saw him, we would share a brief glance and I would exit stage left. He never said anything to me about that night, and neither did I. I hated that I humanized him and left him thinking that somehow it was okay. I took all the blame and carried it with me like my own personal headstone. Thoughts of *For Colored Girls* by Ntosake Shange reminded me that the Boogeyman doesn't lurk in the shadows; he isn't hiding behind a parked car waiting to attack. He's the guy you know, the one you've shared an umbrella with, the one who says hi each morning. I knew him, and from that day forward, I forgot me.

Chapter 1

Hungah

Zee

It was Sunday evening, and I couldn't wait to head over to my girlfriend's house for our weekly book club meeting. This month we were reading Hunter Williams' *Charm Town.* Our club was on book two of the trilogy and we all had so much to share. I cherished these weekly get-togethers. Not only were we able to read and discuss our perspectives on a bestseller, but it was a time for me to share some black girl magic. One of the women there owned an online shoe company, where the shoes were all handmade in Italy. Another woman was a fitness and nutritional guru and had a passion for teaching woman and men how to live our best lives, another club member had a film premiering in the Sundance Film Festival in January, and yet another club member was a budding writer, and we all eagerly waited for her to let us know when we could expect the release date of her novel. We came from all different backgrounds: teachers, college professors, guidance counselors, cosmetologists, social workers, grad students, etc. All who knew that if one of us could find happiness in all the turmoil we face, we all won, and somehow drew collective energy from that success. The plentiful food and drinks also served as a reason to fellowship with one another. The conversations were always rich and colorful, full of life, and a rhythm that only black woman could evoke. Your occasional "Yazzzzzzz" and "Gurllllllll," as well as a sprinkle of "Bitch!" and "Hold up" or "Tell it" were a part of a vernacular that we all understood and loved, one where no manual was needed.

As we wrapped up the night, I was gathering my things, contemplating the work week ahead. As a professor at the local community college, the syllabus is already written. The powers that be allowed me to add some adjustments, but essentially, it was very well scripted. I had plans, however, of becoming tenured at a four-year university soon and then perhaps returning as the president of the community college in the next five to eight years. Taking doctoral classes at the local university in Community College Leadership had helped me to be well on my way to fulfilling my dreams. Tomorrow was an important day. We would all be ready to meet the Associate Director of our department. The last person who held the position was incompetent and under qualified, but I sure hoped this one would be different. I wanted to make sure that I made a good first impression.

The night was long, as most nights are for me. I have had to take sleeping pills to help with my insomnia for years. As I cursed myself for not setting my alarm correctly, and was therefore running late to my first faculty meeting with the new director, I quickly raced up the grand staircase and paused before entering the conference room. I caught my breath at the top of the steps and thought if this new guy is anything like the last one, we were bound not to start on time. The department members were all probably all eating donuts and conversing, while the ass kissers tried to cozy up to the new boss. I was wrong. Terribly wrong. I entered the room and the Dean was in full presentation mode. The lights were bright as if he were on stage. Well, maybe he won't even notice that I am walking in twenty minutes late. I thought, I will just try to make my way to the nearest available seat around this long-ass conference table. Wrong again. Terribly wrong. It was like the door slammed shut for the first time and everyone caught whiplash turning their heads to see who the culprit was as I walked in. "Nice of you to join us, Ms. Warren, please find a seat."

This egotistical bastard, I thought, who in the hell does he think he is, calling me out like that? I was a gangsta in my head, but in reality, my ass took the closest available seat and tried to avoid eye contact. I could hear the mumbles and rumbles, the sounds and stares of disapproval.

"Please, Ms. Warren, please share with us, what was so pressing that you couldn't make it here on time?"

Was he serious? Did he really just ask me to justify my lateness? I stared at him with a puzzled look. I knew he couldn't possibly expect me to answer. Wrong yet again. I was three for three this morning. I could see Candice, the Dean's administrative assistant, feverishly taking notes. The sound her pen made on the paper made me wonder if she would ever enter the technological age. I could hear Lance and Tracy begin to whisper how they wish they could record this whole episode. I could feel the eyes on my back from the others members of the department sitting around the table.

"We are waiting, Ms. Warren."

"Um, well, I just had some…I mean, a slight emergency this morning," I lied.

I clearly was not going to let him know that I didn't set my alarm properly. Please, God, let this be over, I thought with every fiber in my body. I knew that this would be the topic around the proverbial water cooler for weeks to come.

"Ms. Warren, be sure to see me once the meeting is over." The dean's words forced me to look at him and nod. "As I was saying, before Johnny-come-lately decided to join us, this is a new day. We must all remember that we need to serve and meet our students where they are and take them where we want them to be. Just because they are here at our institution of higher learning instead of a four-year college does not mean they deserve any less. I expect for this department of professors to take this job just as seriously as you would any faculty position, and I always inspect what I expect. I will hold you accountable for your actions, so please think long and hard, if this is the place for you. I am about the business of moving our students forward and giving them the best opportunity to succeed. I hope you are too."

I could see that we had a regular Barack Obama "Yes We Can" wannabe leading our way, and I already couldn't stand his guts. The meeting wrapped up, and I hung around the room to save face, but to also do some damage control. I needed to know if it was as bad as I thought it was, and as I spoke with my more trusted colleagues, I was reminded that it was.

"Girl, he laid into that ass, didn't he?" Tracy said, with all the dramatics a comment like that deserved.

"I bet that ass won't be late again," another chimed in.

I had to remind myself that I was in a room full of professionals, who were acting like juveniles without any college degrees. I laughed it off the best I could, and tested the waters of going to HR to complain. I wanted to gauge how much support I may potentially have. Before I could fully explore the idea, I was summoned to the Dean's office. Lord knows I did not want to go in, I was in no mood for another tongue lashing from this dude bent on flexing his academic muscles, and holding his title over my head. As I walked to his office, I could feel the same stares and hear the same whispers of those in the meeting. Word had spread fast, and now colleagues and staff from other departments were chiming in on the morning's events. I entered slowly, but put on my best game face.

"You wanted to see me?"

"Yes, Ms. Warren. Please come in."

I came in and immediately noticed how differently his office was laid out in comparison to the last dean. Pictures of pivotal African-American leaders, like X, King, Evers, Garvey, and Ali lined the walls, as well as literary greats, like August Wilson, Lorraine Hansberry and *Native Son*'s Richard Wright. Quotes from some of my favorite novels were also strategically placed throughout the room like: *What Happens to a Dream Deferred?*, by Langston Hughes; *Ego Trippin'* by Nikki Giovanni; and *Still I Rise* by Maya Angelou were the anchors that held the room together. The room was inviting and warm. The walls had been painted a soothing navy blue with white trim. Small area rugs adorned the entrance and middle of the office. I felt welcomed, although I didn't think I was. The room smelled like a day spa, clean and refreshing, like a springtime rain shower, or freshly done laundry. The walls captivated me, and held my gaze for longer than I expected. It was in this moment that I really looked at the new dean. His eyes were dark and brooding, but held softness in the corners, they were a soothing brown that seem to jump out of his skin. His dark skin melted over me a thousand times over, his full beard only accentuated his strong cheekbones and perfect nose. His broad shoulders were what dreams were made of, impeccably dressed in pleated designer pants and a polo button down shirt that had me begging to be one of the buttons. He stood tall and loomed over me as I tried to keep my composure while entering his office. I stood in front of his desk, taking the only stand I could to resist him by not sitting down. The power of the fish is in the water, and I would be damned if I had him try to navigate mine.

"So, Ms. Warren, I hope that you gathered today that I don't take too kindly to anyone coming in late to my meetings. Please see to it that it doesn't happen again."

It took all I had not to clear curse this brotha out. Is he crazy, or out of his mind? But my "in head" gangsta could talk all she wants, I had a plan, and I wasn't about to ruin it because of a misunderstanding.

"Dean Foster, I do apologize, but was it really necessary to call me out like that? I mean we are all adults here, I don't think it was necessary to take away from the meeting in such a manner."

"You already took away from the meeting when you walked in late. That told me a few things about you. It said that you don't take this work seriously, that you don't respect other people's time, and that meeting your new boss is not a priority for you."

I could tell that arguing with this man was pointless. He was not going to budge, so I conceded.

"Again, I apologize. It won't happen again. Was there anything else?" I needed to get the hell out of this office, before I smacked the shit out this pompous nigga.

He stood up behind his desk once more, and I all but melted into my shoes.

"No, Ms. Warren, that is all for now."

With that, I damn near raced out of the office. I needed to get to my classroom, and teach my English 101 class, and I needed this day to be over. I just wanted to get through it. It still burned a hole in me that the first impression I left on Dean Foster was one of a teacher who didn't care about her job or her students. I waited patiently for 1:15 P.M. to roll around so I could go to lunch and call my best girlfriends, Teka and Constance, to tell them about this unforgettable morning. I sat at my desk in an office I shared with several other professors and graded the batch of papers I had before me. I could smell him before I looked up. My goodness, what did he want from me? Blood? I mean damn, I already apologized. Does he want to see me grovel? Was he going to set the process in motion to have me removed? Was I going to be a target all semester? What? A million scenarios ran through my mind.

"Ms. Warren."

Stay calm, Z. "Yes, Dean Foster, how can I help you?"

"How about lunch?" he responded without ever flinching.

This man can't be for real. Is his ass serious? I thought. I mean he belittles and embarrasses me in front of my colleagues, and now he wants to chop it up over lunch as if this morning never happened. "Um, well, I don't know," I managed to say.

"Come on, my treat, maybe we can start over. I think we both need a redo," he responded.

He was right, I did need one. I couldn't afford to not be on the side of my boss. I needed to change the narrative he had written about me and try to remain in his good graces in order to fulfill my long-term goals.

"Okay," I agreed. "Where did you have in mind?" I asked.

"There is a spot not too far from here that just opened up. Black owned, soul vegan spot called Kemet that I discovered not too long ago."

"Okay. I will meet you there," I offered.

"Really, Ms. Warren? We can ride there together, I promise I won't bite," he responded.

"I don't ride with men I don't know," I asserted, trying to regain some of the power he stripped from me this morning.

"But you know me," he countered.

After the look I gave him told him I was dead serious, he let it go. I was pleased.

"Okay. I will meet you there," he relented.

After an eventful lunch, I felt better about my day. Dean Foster may not be the asshole I had pegged him out to be after all. Our conversation stayed pretty surface level, he was also an HBCU alum, a proud graduate of North Carolina Central, and a southern transplant from New York City. His swag was effortless. He didn't even have to try. It just came naturally for him. He cracked jokes at the appropriate time, spoke with conviction at other times, without missing a beat. The way he spoke about his ambitions, his passion for students at the college level, and his determination to play a vital role in the shaping of the future, almost had me spellbound. Almost. I still held a little bit of a grudge from the morning encounter, and I guess it showed.

"So how long you gonna stay mad?" he asked.

"Wait, what? What do you mean?" He had caught me off guard once again. He was good at it.

"Don't do that," he continued. "You are a smart girl. How long are you gonna be salty? You were wrong, Ms. Warren. Just take responsibility for your actions, and let's move on. I am willing to do so if you are."

"I am," I said halfheartedly.

"Don't say it if you don't mean it. Look, we have a chance to really make a difference in the lives of young adults. I really hope that we are on the same page. I have to ensure that everyone on my team understands that I mean business when it comes to this. There is too much at stake. I need everyone to be clear that I am spirited and vehemently committed to this work."

"Okay, I understand and I share your enthusiasm, but it doesn't have to be all or nothing. It doesn't mean severing trust before it has even been established to prove a point. The same people or person who you need on your team may be the same people or person you alienate with your 'all hands on deck' leadership style. It wouldn't hurt to just show people you're human, and understand that sometimes things happen and people run late." There, I said it.

"People? Or just you? Look, I invited you to lunch because I wanted to start again. If you are going to hold this over my head for the rest of the semester just let me know now."

He didn't miss a step. Every word seemed calculated. Yet, his smile filled with those pearly whites could be what made me forgive him indefinitely. I could suck on those lips all night long. I was suddenly hungry. Not hungry for the vegan tofu sandwich that was sitting in front of me, but for this man. This beauty of a man, sitting across from me, in all of his majestic glory. Sexiness oozing from every pore of his body. How could someone I just met, less than six hours earlier be giving me such chills, already. I had already pictured him naked, I had already pictured him with me. How could this be, I didn't even know this man.

"I was just a little taken aback," I chimed back into reality. "But I am on your team, and I do want what is best for the students. I am willing to move on."

"Bet," he answered.

"How do you do that?"

"Do what?" Dean answered.

"Go back and forth with your Dean Foster language, and your 'round the way vernacular."

"You know how we do, I am sure you do it as well, constantly moving between both worlds."

"Yeah, I get it," I admitted.

As we sat at the table, our conversation moved to everything from old school hip-hop to the politics of Community College education, and it seemed to flow with ease. I was so enamored by his vast knowledge of things that I thought were my own secret. My love for Khalil Gibran, Paulo Coelho and African Proverbs

class, and was all but ready to pack up and walk out the door. What a day it had been. As I made my way down the long corridor and rounded the corner, I couldn't help but to peek into the room where Dean Foster's office was located. I spotted him. He was making small talk with his secretary, or perhaps giving orders in his fashion. How dare he come here and walk all over my mind without a care. Where were all my carefully placed guards that I had mounted around my mind and heart when it came to men like him? I don't know how he was having such an effect on me. Reason and sensibility went out the door, when it came to him. I didn't notice a ring on his finger, and he hadn't talked about a significant other over lunch. But maybe it was too soon to get into real personal business. This man had only been here a day, and had already managed to throw me completely off my game. I needed to recoup. Maybe call one of my cuddle buddies to warm my bed tonight. I knew it would all be in vain, I would only be thinking about Dean Foster through the whole five minutes of extreme passion and pleasure. I scurried along, not wanting to make eye contact, too late. Dean Foster turned around and his eyes met mine. I was lost in them. I tried to swim my way out, to reach land before he engulfed me without saying a word. Did he know? Jesus, Z! You only went out to lunch, it was only a simple hug. I had to stop reading more to it than what it plainly was. Nothing. He smiled and waved goodnight. I waved back and continued my trek to the elevator. Before pulling off and out of the parking garage, I sat in my car and thought of him. I thought about his mind, his body, his confidence. I thought about what it would be like to be with him. I knew this man would be the start of something amazing or the start of something tumultuous. Either way I thought I was willing to find out.

Dean Foster

Zenia Warren. My goodness. God was showing off when he made her. Her dark melanated skin, high cheekbones, piecing brown eyes and neat black dreadlocks that reached the small of her back was enough to make any man lose his mind. She was a sight to behold. I made it a point to know who all my teachers were before starting any job, and I couldn't help but to know who she was. She was ambitious, and goal orientated, taking on more classes than she really had to, just to strengthen her skill set. A graduate of Florida A&M University and a master's degree from the University of Maryland. This woman seemed to have it all. Brains, beauty and drive. She was self-motivated and a definite leader, but I would be damned if she would disrespect me by coming in to my meeting, a meeting she knew about well in advance, over twenty minutes late. Who the hell did she think she was! I know I was probably a little too hard on her, and may have went a bit overboard with having her explain her tardiness, but I learned a long time ago, if you want to make a statement, make it early. I had to let her and all her colleagues know that I would not tolerate lack of respect for the work we do. If that was too much for her, so be it. I am glad I got a chance to take her to lunch. The whole time, I couldn't do anything but admire her well fitted tan A-line skirt that accentuated her thick frame. The silk blouse that cascaded just enough to show the very top of her brown breasts. Those thighs, those hips, I could tell she didn't skip many meals. Her thickness hung in all the right places. Her voluptuous lips had me going wild on the inside. But what intrigued me more than anything was our conversation. I could actually talk to her about a variety of issues, not just work, not just social issues. It wasn't more than a little over an hour, but that was all I needed to solidify the fact that I had to be in her life. I had to make her mine. I would do anything to get to know her, all of her in every way possible. There was no time like the present. I hadn't asked for her number, but figured I would be bold and call her anyway. It wasn't as if it was hard to find. My secretary kept a directory of all the faculty. As I sat at home with her number between my fingers, I contemplated maybe being more traditional and asking her for her number the next time I saw her at work, but fuck it, no time like the present.

"Hello, is this Ms. Warren?"

"May I ask who's calling, please?" her voice smooth and sultry.

"You may," I answered.

"Oh, so you want to play games, I am going to hang this phone up," she said playfully.

"No, you're not, because I know you have caller ID and so you know who this is," I asserted.

"Dean Foster."

"Why are you calling me? How did you get my number?" she asked.

"Nevermind. Is everything okay or are you calling to remind me not to be late to your next meeting?" she added, full of sarcasm.

"Oh, so you got jokes, huh?" I countered.

I decided to go all in. "You don't want me to call you?"

Silence.

"Answer me."

Oh, Lord, this man just oozed confidence from his very pores. LAWD, it turned me on. Zee thought to herself practically, out loud.

"I mean, I don't mind you calling, it's just, you know, you could have been a gentleman and asked for my number. I may have given it to you." she said.

"I could have. What are you doing right now?"

"About to eat this popcorn and watch the latest episode of *Insecure*. Why?" she asked.

"The night is young, I figured we can head on down to Adams Morgan in D.C. and catch some poetry, maybe a few drinks, you game?"

"Well, I'm not sure, don't know if I feel like driving to D.C. tonight." she said hesitantly.

"You don't have to drive," I said trying to convince her.

"I already told you, I don't ride with—" I cut her off abruptly.

"I know, men you don't know, but damn, girl, we done went out to lunch, we had a disagreement, I hugged you, we are practically married."

She couldn't help but laugh. I know she was thinking that I was a trip.

"Look, I am not trying to intimidate you or scare you, but I am new in town and I just want to go out with someone who I think I am going to have a good time with, maybe laugh a little, listen to some amazing poetry, and do a little dancing. Is there any harm in that?" I was laying it on thick.

'No, I guess not," she said. "Okay, give me about an hour or so to get ready, you got a girl thinking she was chilling with Issa Rae tonight."

"You can record it," I said.

"I guess. See you in a bit." she finally relented.

$\mathcal{Z}ee$

After giving him my address, I hung up the phone, and let out a light scream. It was like I was a teenager that was just asked to the prom by the captain of the football team. Dean Foster wanted to be in my company. I hadn't planned on going out, but figured I could whip together something nice in no time. Something sexy but not too revealing. I elected to go with my Betty, Angela and Ida Taught Me, black t-shirt and denim jeans with my black knee-high leather boots. I wore my leather hip-length jacket with the faux fur around the collar. I wore my name plate for good measure, and some gold hoop earrings. I brought along my poetry book, just in case we caught an open mic and I got the spirit to show Dean Foster who he was working with! I showered and put my dreadlocks up into a high bun. I applied minimal makeup not wanting to look too desperate. I think my outfit matched the itinerary for the night. I must have paced around the room a thousand times. As I waited, I called my girlfriend Teka for a little sista reassurance.

"So you must really be feeling this dude."

"I know right, I mean I just met him, but it's like we can hang out forever."

"Damn, girl, this nigga got your nose wide open, what kind of spell did he put on you? I have never seen you like this before."

"Girl, I can't believe it either. Where they do that at? Why am I going out with him, like he just called me out of the blue?"

"It wasn't out of the blue, you both were feeling a connection and he couldn't resist. Just go for it for once in your life, Z. Damn. Just bring your mace and pepper spray just in case the nigga act crazy." She laughed. But it was no joking matter to me. Ever since college, I had tried to be extra careful as to who I allowed in my space. I never wanted to be put in a position of utter helplessness again. Then here comes Dean Foster, sauntering into my life and making me feel like I have no control. I was ready to take a risk, and it would have to be with him."

Exactly an hour and a half later, Mr. Dean Foster stood at my door ringing my bell. I opened up and was pleasantly pleased with what I saw. Dark blue trench coat. Black jeans and nice pair of boots. Wool cap that made his gorgeous features and beard stand out even more. Give me strength tonight, Lord.

"Hello, Dean Foster. Come on in, let me grab my bag and turn off the TV in my room."

"Okay." He walked, more like strolled in with the bop that black men posses, when they make even the simple act of walking seem ultra-cool. "Nice place."

I know he was eying my life size poster of Assata Shakur and Queen Nzingha and my framed words of Jesse Williams' famed speech from the 2016 BET Awards. When I entered back into the living room, there he stood in front of my bookcase thumbing through the pages of one of my manuscripts that I had written and bound from a graduate creative writing class.

"So you are a writer as well, huh, my very own Sista Souljah," he laughed.

"I like to think of myself more in the realm of Alice Childress."

"Oh, okay, Alice in Wonderland. Well, are you ready to have some fun?"

"Yes, indeed."

The ride to D.C. was filled with who had the more classic of classic albums, my choice of Nas' *Illmatic* or his of Jay Z's *Reasonable Doubt*, Michael Jackson's *Thriller*, or Prince's *Purple Rain*, and of course dissecting every song in Stevie Wonders' classic, *Songs in the Key of Life*. It was nice to not have to always talk about politics or work, sometimes you just wanted to unwind and talk about things that in most eyes didn't matter, but I liked that it mattered to him. I wrote one of my thesis papers in graduate school on Lauryn Hill's *Miseducation* album. It was peppered with the often misguided and misunderstood lives of young black women in America. I shared with him my disillusionment that black girls are four times more likely to be arrested at school and seven times more likely to be suspended than their white peers. This often means that the misguided perceptions of black girls start early. Therefore, what happens to those same black girls as they matriculate into society as young adults? No one really looks out for them, we are the most unprotected, undervalued, and misrepresented faction of society. It ultimately leads to black women living up to those stereotypes or not knowing how to properly deal with our issues. He disagreed, with some of my sentiments, pointing out how black women have made great strides in education, politics and fashion, and we were able to have a heart filled discussion on the topic.

At the poetry joint, we listened to some great up and coming poets, as well as some amateurs and I sipped on my favorite drink, Amaretto Sour, while he drank a Guinness. We danced to the rhythm of a live band and I was feeling like Nia Long in *Love Jones*. On our way back to the car we stopped by the best pizza place in D.C., where the slices reminded Dean of New York Style Pizzerias. We laughed as we noted how gentrified so many places in D.C. had become. Places that in the past you wouldn't be caught walking after 5:00 P.M. and now have several coffee shops, thrift stores and great places to buy a green smoothie. We laughed to keep from crying and making the night too somber with all the oppression and obstacles our people felt on a daily basis.

As we pulled back into my long driveway, Dean Foster walked out to open my door. What a gentleman. As he took my hand to help me out he pulled me close to him and held me in a tight embrace. I could live in that cocoon forever. I was too afraid to pull away, not wanting to meet his eyes. Afraid of what I may feel. I couldn't be that girl. The girl who gave up the goods to a guy I just met the same day. I mean, I read *Think like a Man*. I knew about the ninety-day rule. I found it archaic in nature. I knew several women who had sex on the first day or first week of meeting someone, and lived a full life and seemed to be pretty happy. Some of them even ended up marrying the guy they slept with.

He pulled back and lifted my head toward him by placing his fingers underneath my chin.

"Tell me what you are thinking right now," he commanded, not asked.

"I am thinking I had a really nice time with you, and would love to do it again sometime."

"That is all you're thinking about?" he responded.

"Look, it's been a long day. I need to get in the house and get some sleep before I have to take the day off tomorrow, and if you don't like lateness, I know you damn sure don't like absences."

"Don't do that."

"Don't do what?"

"C'mon, we both grown. Tell me what you are really thinking at this very moment."

"You know what, why don't you tell me what's on your mind?" I challenged. I would not let this man get me all rattled and speaking like I didn't know how to string a sentence together.

"Damn, Z, we are not in high school, you don't have to pretend. I mean, I am thinking I would love to take you into this house and fuck the shit out of you. I want to taste you, I want to make you come over and over again, I want to kiss you from your head to your toes. I want to make love to you all night long, I want your lips all over me, I want you to suck and fuck my brains out. I want to wake up next to you in the morning and do it all over again. That's what I'm thinking."

Damn, I need to be careful about what I ask!

"Who do you think you are?" I said. My voice laced with feigned indignation.

"A man who knows and gets what he wants," he replied.

"Okay, well, I hate to disappoint you, because all of that is not happening."

"So look at me and tell me you weren't thinking the same thing."

"I wasn't."

"Don't lie to me, don't ever lie to me. Just tell me you were thinking the same thing."

"You are not going to bully me into telling you what you want to hear. I was not thinking the same thing," I lied. "I am sure that is hard for you to understand, as you probably have women swooning over you, dying to jump in bed with you, well, guess what? Maybe you should have called one of them tonight."

"Oh, so now I'm a bully? And you're right, I do have my pick of women wanting to have sex with me. There is nothing wrong with that. I am a grown-ass man. I make choices in my life that I can deal with. Being an adult is about making adult choices. And for a woman who is so into such literary giants, who had no problem exposing their soul, and living in the moment, you can't answer a simple question honestly. Just answer the question. Are you feeling me or not?"

"I can't right now."

"What are you so afraid of?"

"Why I got to be afraid? Did you ever stop to think that maybe I just don't want to be another score in your concubine of ladies you've conquered in one day? Or maybe I do not want to sleep with someone I have to work with? I was raised to respect myself."

"Oh, I see, so if you sleep with me tonight, you don't respect yourself? Nevermind the fact that we are both two consenting adults, obviously attracted to one another who may happen to also like sex. We don't have to fit or conform to society's rules of when that should happen. We don't have to follow a timeline."

"Okay, I am too tired to go back and forth with you. I just want to call it a night, and still leave with some respect for myself and for you."

"Oh, don't worry, sweetheart, you gonna always show me respect."

In this very moment, there was a slight fracture in the pedestal I had placed him on. He was overbearing, rude and obnoxious and it was starting to frustrate the living daylight out of me. I realized in that moment that because I focused on the snake, I missed the scorpion. This man's tongue was like a million poisonous bites.

"All right, you win, Dean Foster. You win. You're right, as my boss, I will respect you, but right now, you are the one who's going to have to respect my wishes, and that includes me going into my house, to go to sleep alone."

"Absolutely," he replied.

"Goodnight, Dean Foster."

"Goodnight, Ms. Warren."

Chapter 2

Can I Stay with You?
Zee

The next couple of weeks were uneventful. Ever since my date with Dean Foster, we hadn't said more than a few words to one another. The more I was in his presence, the more it became painfully clear, that I was infatuated by the thought of him, not the actual person I had come to know on our date. I was still madly attracted to him, but none of that mattered. He had moved on to other things. I guess I didn't intrigue him as much anymore either. We hadn't been on another lunch outing as he promised, and every time I saw him around campus or in our department building we never had more than a casual hello, or superficial inquiries into how we both were doing. Besides, today I was focused on one thing: getting my idea picked up for the new elective class in the Spring. Every year, faculty members are encouraged to submit their proposal for a class they would like to develop and facilitate in the upcoming fall semester. It is fashioned after Genius

Hour at Google, where the employees are able to share their ideas and how they would like to develop them. This was the college's attempt to foster more trust between professors and leadership, and foster an environment where all thoughts and opinions mattered. It was cost effective, and only offered as an elective; therefore, it did not interfere with the required course of study for most of our students. Some of the courses were even offered during the weekend or online. It also served as a way for professors to develop their research for advanced degrees, and sharpen their skills. It created more buy in from the teaching community and served as great advertisement for our small college. These meetings have produced such classes like "The Words and Times of Tupac Shakur," "The Psychology of Adult ADHD," and many more. As long as the professor could tie in writing and essential reading comprehension skills into the course, and relate everything back to the required standards of our educational model, any idea could be considered. I had been working on my proposal all semester and only needed the vote of two-thirds of the faculty and the Dean. The final step was the approval of the Community College president. I already knew, based on my relationship with several of my colleagues that I had at least half of them on board with my idea. I sincerely thought I could persuade the rest, and I naturally assumed that Dean Foster would be on my side. I mean wasn't it him who stated that he was here for the best interest of the students. At the conference table I laid out my proposal, entitled "The Revolution Will Not Be Televised," examining the writings of Sam Green Lee, Olaudah Equiano, and Frantz Fanon. The vote came in and I was surprised that some of my colleagues who had pledged allegiance to my idea earlier in the semester were not voting for the class. Finally, Dean Foster said his piece:

"I really don't see how this class is different from some of the courses we currently offer," his voice stern and cold.

I was shocked. Was this man really shooting down my idea?

"Yes," another professor added. "Don't we offer writing classes that focus on some of these authors already?"

I felt like a mother who was having a baby ripped out of her arms. I had to fight for my idea. I had to find my voice. "Well, actually, some courses may take a superficial look at Fanon, but it is not done in the context I will be presenting it in," I asserted.

"And what context would that be, Ms. Warren?" Dean Foster replied. This nigga was so close from me leaping across the table and knocking the shit out of him. All eyes were on me, they were waiting for my cool and collected response. I was once again letting someone else control the narrative. The eyes shifted from staring at me to staring down at the papers before them. It was an uncomfortable silence. The room seemed to become smaller and smaller. The stale off-white paint on the walls seemed to be deathly close to my skin. The chair I was sitting on all of sudden felt so rigid, as if the cushion was no longer there to support me. The tapping of a pen in the hand of one of my colleagues was masquerading as a ticking time bomb. It was as if everything was moving in slow motion. I made eye contact with Dean Foster, hoping he would be able to see the desperation in my eyes. I was hoping he could feel my earnest plea for him to defend me by supporting and accepting my proposal. I was waiting on him to use his savvy charm and wit, to turn this whole situation around. I needed him to throw me a life saver. I was drowning in despair and humiliation. That moment didn't come. Instead he met my gaze, and never once averted his eyes. He was looking right at me and through me, perhaps waiting on me to assert my position, to straighten my back up and defend my idea. He may have been waiting for me to use all of my fancy degrees in rhetoric and English Composition to get a handle on what was happening in the room.

I tried my best to explain that the context of my course included how the resistance against the establishment was best vocalized through the voices of these writers. In addition, *The Spook Who Sat by the Door,* by Sam GreenLee, was a virtual blueprint on how a modern day revolution could take place. It seemed like the more I spoke, the more he shot me down. He reminded me that the revolution that takes place in GreenLee's novel juxtaposed to today's highly technological society would be practically impossible, and that students would never be able to make the connection. He surmised that the idea was far reaching and whimsical at best. Dean Foster reminded everyone that it was not the college's job to shape or impose our own political opinions on students. Instead, he shared, that our mission was not to develop revolutionaries, but students who were critical thinkers, who understood the curriculum, and developed the knowledge and skills to be competitive in the workforce after they left our halls. I couldn't believe this was happening. My mind was literally blown away. I never pegged Dean Foster for the type of person who didn't think outside the box. If all education was to him was the rote memorization of facts, and theories that had already been tested and proven, then what type of critical thinkers would we produce? The mindset was completely fixed. It was business as usual. Great ideas aren't born and developed if everyone just follows the status quo. I thought our job was to challenge conventional thinking.

Despite my best efforts, at the end of the meeting, my idea for a fall elective was tabled for another time, which essentially meant that it would not be picked up. I felt like Dean Foster had punched me in the stomach. Was this his way of getting back at me for not giving in to his advances? I knew I would have to find out before the day was over. The thought of having to mull this over in my mind all night until tomorrow ate at my core. I have never been a person who liked confrontation, unless I felt it was absolutely necessary and could not be avoided. I reasoned, however, that it was better to face this situation head on.

At the end of the afternoon, after most classes had either been dismissed or were in session, and before my 6 P.M. class, I made my way over to Foster's office. I felt like a prisoner walking the last mile. I kept thinking about the earlier session and practiced some of the points that I failed to make clear. I wanted to be given another chance to convince Dean Foster and my colleagues, that they had somehow made a mistake in their voting earlier. I was looking particularly put together today, since I knew I would be presenting my proposal. A black, well-fitted Donna Karan pantsuit, paired with a low-cut gold blouse with a single black button that sat perfectly at the top of my chest. The pants and the jacket really helped to show off my curves. It made my apple bottom sit high and accentuated my waist. The room in the pants leg was just right. It wasn't too tight, but definitely made an impression. I realized a long time ago that my body was not going to conform to the beauty standards I was inundated with as a child. I had to train my mind to appreciate my melanin, my curves and my hair. I loved that my hair grew upward toward the sun and that my skin radiated in the summertime. I especially loved that now, after years of torment, ridicule and being made fun of for my full lips and butt, many women were paying enormous amounts of money to have what I was born with. Attending an HBCU definitely help to normalize who I was.

I bypassed the secretary, walking briskly and dared her to stop me. I could hear her ask if I had an appointment, but I ignored her inquiry and remained steadfast on my mission. If I would have stopped to talk to her, I would have lost the courage to confront Dean Foster. I knocked and opened the door to his office at the same time. I knew that would piss him off, but I didn't care. I needed answers.

"What the hell is wrong with you?" he exclaimed as I entered into his space. Fresh on my heels was the secretary, letting the Dean know that I proved to be a formidable force to try to stop. He excused her and she left the room.

I tried to remain focused on my goal. "What's wrong with me? What the hell is wrong with you?"

ing me long enough to grab my face with his thumb on one side and the other four fingers on the other.

"You miss me?"

I didn't want to go there with him. I just wanted to continue feeling good. Why did he have to find a way to complicate things?

"You miss me?" he asked again, this time his eyes demanding an answer. 'Tell the truth, Z. If you missed me, say you missed me."

I didn't want to be vulnerable, but I could no longer deny what I was feeling for this man. I decided to find a piece of me that day, right there in his arms.

"I missed you."

"Say it again."

"I missed you," I repeated.

"Do you want me?"

"I...."

"Then tell me you want me."

This man was going to make me beg.

"You know I do."

"The last I checked you were hell bent on making sure you respected yourself. Remember that?" he reminded me. "Answer me," he demanded.

"Yes, I remember," I managed to say.

"What's changed?"

"Why are you doing this? Do you want me to beg? Is that it? You have a sick fetish of seeing women bow down at your feet. You won't be satisfied until you break me? You know, I am feeling a mix of emotions right now."

"Exactly. Therefore, I just want to make sure that this is what you want."

"What? I am in here now."

"Yeah, that you are, but I don't think you came here with the intention of us being intimate with one another. Did you?" he asked.

I couldn't answer, because I wasn't quite sure of the response I would give.

"Listen, why don't you go ahead and take the rest of the evening off. It's Friday. I will be sure to let the students in your 6 P.M. class know that tonight's session is cancelled."

"I don't need or want your pity. I can teach my class," I said.

"It's okay to accept my help, really, it is. I don't want anything in return. The world won't collapse because you missed one class. Please, Ms. Warren, just go ahead and go home."

I reluctantly took Dean Foster's advice. Maybe I did need to take some time to clear my head. On my way home I picked up some wine with plans to drown my sorrows, while taking a nice relaxing bubble bath. My, how the events in the past few weeks have made my head spin. On top of everything else, including my newly found lack of confidence from having my hard work overlooked today, I opened up today and let my true feelings be known to Dean Foster, and what did it get me? A suggestion to go home early. I got home and couldn't make my mind think of anything but that kiss, that embrace, that man. He had my head in the clouds and now I wanted him more than ever. I remember he shared with me where he lived that night we painted the town red in D.C. I went against my better judgment and decided I wouldn't spend another night without him by my side. He made my problems seem so manageable. I put on my sexiest bra and panty set, a trench coat and decided it was now or never. I was ready to quench this burning desire that I had for him tonight. My hands were shaking the entire drive to Dean Foster's house. My heart felt like it was beating one hundred beats per minute. My palms became sweaty as I pulled into his driveway. There could be a possibility that he turned me away, or worse yet, his significant other answered the door. I figured I already bared part of my soul to this man, so another bold move, would be the next logical step. He had seen me at one of my lowest points professionally, and the way we kissed, the way he held me had to mean something. I got out of the car, and quickly made my way to his front door.

I rang the bell. I could hear his footsteps come to the door.

"Who is it?"

"It's me, Zee."

He came to the door with a white t-shirt and gray sweatpants. His muscles bulging. His chest rock hard. His dark skin gleaming juxtaposed to the shirt he was wearing. Both hands in his pockets, he stood tall, his legs slightly apart. A sight to behold. Even in everyday causal lounge wear, this man could be on the cover of *GQ* magazine.

He looked at me for a moment and let out a long sigh. "What are you doing here?" he asked sternly.

"I had to see you," I replied.

"Really? You had to see me? So you don't own a phone anymore, is that it? You just show up to a man's house unannounced?"

I could feel the tension in his voice rising.

"What do you think is going to happen now, Zee, huh?" The crescendo was at the tip of his lips. "Who the fuck do you think you are? Is this the way it happens in your favorite movie? Boy meets girl, girl has a meltdown, and goes rushing into the arms of the man, because this is real life and you have no right coming over here without letting me know first?"

So far, this was not looking promising. He was genuinely pissed off. I had to try to calm him down, so he could see my true intentions.

"I know it looks crazy…."

"No, Zee, it doesn't look crazy, it is crazy," he interrupted. "I did not invite you over here. You just can't do what the hell you want to do, when you feel like it, just because you had a rough day. That's not how shit works, you got a lot of damn nerve coming to my house. What if I had someone over here?"

"I just wanted to see you, I needed to see you."

"I have things to do, this shit is too much." He began to close the door.

"Wait, please. Today, you asked me if I wanted you. I do, Dean, I've wanted you from the first time I met you. I want to see where this can go. Can I stay with you tonight?" I damn near pleaded.

I could tell he was contemplating the question over and over in his mind. After a brief pause, he moved to the side and allowed me to come in. After he closed the door behind him, he sat on the sofa while I stood in front of him. I took off my trench coat. He didn't say a word. He didn't need to. I moved closer to him and straddled his lap. I kissed his eyes, his cheeks his nose, his forehead, his lips. I sucked on his ear lobes, and let my fingers play in his full beard. He quickly removed my bra and grabbed both breasts and acted as if they were his nighttime snack. He placed butterfly kisses on each breast before placing the right breast in his mouth and used his thumb to caress and massage the left nipple. The shit was enough to send me flying like a rocket.

"I want you, Dean Foster, I want you so bad," I assured him.

He grabbed a fistful of my dreadlocks, and pulled my head back so that I could look directly into his eyes. "I demand a lot from the woman that I allow into my life. I don't have time for games," he answered.

"I don't want to play games anymore," I said.

With that, I dropped to my knees. Dean made a quick move to remove his gray sweatpants and underwear. I was not disappointed. His size was everything I thought it would be. Long and thick, I held his manhood in my hands and gently stroked up and down. I kissed and sucked on him like my life depended on it. I could hardly place the entire thing in my mouth. He placed his hand on top of my head and help guide me in and out, up, and down of his hard-on. I used my free hand to get myself excited as well. After a few minutes, he picked me up and placed me on the sofa, his shirt was already on the floor and he wasted no time in ripping my underwear off. He spread my legs apart and began massaging my secret garden with his fingers. I was dripping wet, trembling, and begging for more. He feasted on me for what seemed like forever. I admired the power of his tongue. He licked me into oblivion. His tongue caressing my clit until I felt like I was about to explode. His tongue went in and out and all around my vagina until I couldn't take it anymore. It was like he had taken a master class in giving woman sexual pleasure. He finally came up for air, and placed a trail of kisses from my navel to my lips. I kissed him with everything I had. I needed him to know that this was what I wanted. I needed him to believe me. I wanted him to become one with me, I wanted to feel him inside of me. It was almost like he knew I couldn't take it any longer and wanted his dick inside of me.

"Tell me what you want," he teased.

"I want you, right now, please," I answered.

He began to enter me slowly at first but then faster. As he slid in and out, my sugar walls began to conform to his size, although it was difficult at first. I could feel myself ready to come a thousand times over, and he knew it.

"Hold on, baby, don't come yet, let me take you where you need to be."

"I can't help it, you feel so good, I'm about to co… come," I moaned.

"Not yet, baby, you can't come until I tell you to."

I tried my best to comply. I wanted this feeling to last longer.

"You want me to stop?" he whispered.

"No," I said emphatically.

"Tell me," he said.

"Please don't stop," I begged.

"Damn, baby, you feel so good," his voice warm and smooth.

"Please, baby, let me come, I can't take it."

After a few more strokes, he finally granted my wish. "Go ahead, baby, you can come now, come all over this."

We made love for what seemed like forever, and then he collapsed on top of me. After about twenty minutes we were at it again. We made our way to his bedroom. This time we explored other positions. Me on top, him from behind, him from the side. Each time, he didn't disappoint. I was spent. I kissed him gently on his lips, before dozing off to sleep.

"Goodnight, Dean Foster.'

"Goodnight, Ms. Warren."

$\mathcal{D}$ e a n

What was this spell that this queen had me under? Normally I would never allow a woman to come to my house without letting me know first. Not intentionally, anyway. I was pissed, when I saw her on my door step. Who did she think she was? But one look at her, and I couldn't resist. That wasn't a good sign. That means that she had me in a space, where I didn't control everything. For me, control is paramount. It has always been that way. I needed to regain control. Because of events in my past, I could never let any woman or man feel like they had me eating out the palm of their hands. I would not allow it. To me everything in life was a test. You were constantly being prepped to do something, or you were being judged by your work, looked at with more scrutiny than others because of the color of your skin. I always had to work twice as hard, to get positions that my white counterparts were able to get by calling their frat brother or father for a favor. I have two master's degrees, and a doctorate in College Leadership and Management, and yet, the furthest I have gotten is the Associate director of the Reading Department of a community college. My plan was to become the president of the community college and then go on to lead a four year institution. The icing on the cake would be if that institution was an HBCU. However, those presidents seem like they never leave. And then here comes Ms. Warren, I haven't been able to do my job at 100 percent because I was enamored with her, with everything about her. Her walk, her talk, her hair, the clothes she wears, and the way she moves. I was like a walking Debarge song! In my future plans, I needed a Michelle Obama, by my side. I didn't know if she could fit the bill. I didn't know much about her past, but I never forget what people tell me, and her apprehension for not wanting to ride with men she didn't know made me wonder about what she was hiding. Her meltdown today over her course idea being rejected should have set off some alarms for me. I haven't been in a serious relationship in years. My closest friends will tell you it's because I am waiting for the perfect lady to cross my path. I know women who set standards for themselves all day long. Most are unrealistic. A nigga gotta be handsome, built, great with kids, have a great career, be liked by their girlfriends, loved by their family, have a great job, make good money, be able to read their minds, shower them with gifts, be a hero, a thug, a business man. They wanted it all. Why was it wrong that I wanted a woman on my level as well?

I know I was trying to find a reason to not give this thing with Ms. Warren a chance. I also knew that it was risky business trying to have a serious relationship with someone you worked with. There were a million red flags there. The university had a strict code of professional conduct especially if you happen to hold a position of power over the person you are sleeping with. What if she had planned this night all along? How do I know she didn't set this all up to turn around and charge me with sexual harassment or some shit like that? This must be why she came storming into my office about her class idea that I voted against? She made sure she made a scene in front of my secretary about coming to see me. She was most likely ensuring that she had a credible witness in case this whole thing came before an advisory board. How could I be so stupid? All for what? I can't believe I let myself slip like this.

I looked over and saw that she was still fast asleep on her side. Her beautiful head full of long black, silky dreadlocks cascading down her back, some on the pillow. Her body was so enticing. I wanted to roll her over and pick up where we left off last night. I leaned in close and spooned with her. My excitement was not contained as I gently placed kisses on her bare shoulder.

"Wake up, baby." I wasn't going to be the only one being tested today.

She stirred a bit. I reached down and placed my hand on her ass and massaged it until I knew she was fully awake.

"You think you slick, huh, Ms. Warren?"

"Hmm, what?"

"You heard me, get the fuck up."

She turned around to face me, her big brown eyes wide, and in a state of confusion. I could tell she was trying to figure out if I was joking around, or was serious.

"What are you talking about?"

"You gotta go."

"Are you serious right now? You can't possibly be serious right now. You kicking me out?"

"That's right."

"Wait, what did I do? Where is this coming from? I thought we shared something special," she said. "You thought wrong," I interjected. "Listen, I got a lot of work to do today, and I can't afford to have any distractions." With that, I got up and started putting on my clothes. I threw on some boxers and handed her a clean t-shirt I had in my drawer.

I can tell that tears were starting to form in her eyes. But I couldn't stop. I damn near threw her trench coat at her. I knew she didn't know what to say or to think. Less than ten hours ago, I was making the sweetest love to her, and here I was acting like she was some woman I met on a street corner.

"Wait, Dean, why are you doing this? Please just tell me, talk to me, let me know what I did, did I say something to offend you last night? If I did, I'm sorry. Is it because I came over unannounced? I mean, it won't happen again," she managed to say behind the tears that were now falling freely down her face.

"Look, I am not going to keep repeating myself. I said I have work to do and you gotta go."

"You are a bitch-ass nigga, you know that?"

I could tell she was trying to redeem the little respect she had left. I left her no choice.

"Yeah, okay. Say it again, and see if I don't knock the shit out of you."

She moved quickly, as she looked for her shoes, bra and torn underwear in the living room. I didn't know why I was hurting this woman like this. She had been nothing but kind to me, a familiar face in a new city. It was almost as if I needed to see her grovel, I needed to be in charge. In my mind, it was like she held all the cards, and something in me just wouldn't allow that to be the case. I had convinced myself that last night was too good to be true, and that she was plotting my demise, like so many had done before her.

I stood by the door intentionally so that I could see her as she made her way out to leave. I held her car keys in my hand, which would force her to have to come to me to get them. As she made her way toward me, I could tell she was a mess. It was like I ripped her heart out and stomped on it. She could hardly look at me, when she did, her eyes were red, and she was bewildered, like a deer caught in headlights. I knew she wanted to smack my face with everything she had, but based on my behavior, she also knew there was a strong possibility that I might really fight her back. I don't think that was a risk she was willing to take. She stood before me, and waited for me to hand her keys over. I took my time, almost like torture. This was my way of regaining control. This lady had no idea about my sordid past. She should have known better than to trust anyone so freely. That wasn't my fault. That was hers, I convinced myself. She looked up at me and tried to caress my face. I wanted that touch more than anything in the world but I pushed her hand away. I gave her the keys and opened the door so she could leave. Without saying a word, she said it all. I had broken her, and I knew it.

Chapter 3

Weakness

Zee

I damn near sprinted to my car. Once I got in I burned rubber out of Dean Foster's driveway. I could see him standing by the door as I backed the car out. I waited until I got around the corner, pulled over and put the car in park. I banged on the steering wheel with all the strength I wanted to punch him with. I screamed at the top of my lungs.

"SHITTTTTTTTTTTTT!!! What the FUCK-KKK!!!!" was all I managed to get out. It took so much energy. Why, why, why did I put myself in this position? How could I be so stupid? What was I thinking? A man like Dean Foster could be with anyone, why did I think that he would have anything more than a casual, sexual relationship with me? I could it feel it coming. I haven't had one in quite some time. My anxiety attacks had gotten better these last few months. Not only that, as a person who suffered from severe depression, I took extra caution to appear normal. I was really starting to turn a corner these last few years with my mental health. I needed my pills. With my illness I knew that I could have an extreme mood swing at any time. I could go from feelings of mania, to periods of extreme sadness in a matter of hours. There were times that I experienced both at the same time. I had to make a conscious effort to calm myself down, so that I could safely drive home. I needed to see Dr. Fritz as soon as possible. I took several deep breaths and willed myself to drive home. Once there, I showered, dressed and threw my hair into a ponytail. I took my medicine and made my way to the office of my psychologist. I didn't have an appointment, but this was an emergency. I felt like I was literally losing my mind. I was so happy he held weekend hours, often times I felt as if I lived in his office.

As a waited in the waiting room, I replayed everything back in my head. What did he mean by me trying to be slick? I mean did he not pursue me in the beginning? Did he not lay out a thesis about us being consenting adults and not conforming to society's rules about when was an appropriate time to have sex? This was the same man who needed me to reassure him over and over again that I wanted him, and then, just like that he flips out with no explanation.

Years after my college incident, I decided that I had some things that I could use some help with. The thing about mental health in the black community is, help is seen in different ways, if it is seen or offered at all. Those ways don't always include seeing a professional who can actually give you concrete steps and strategies to improve your life, or taking medication that can help stabilize the dysfunctional neurons in your brain. It becomes even more difficult if you don't have a health insurance plan that covers mental illness or a job that promotes mental health wellbeing. No. Methods to deal with mental health in my family, meant church and praying to Jesus, which is fine, but sometimes God himself is showing you that you may need a mental health counselor, psychologist, or psychiatrist. Help could also be going to an aunt, who practices voodoun. I mean when you grow up with a Haitian mother, sometimes problems are solved that way. And I don't mean, the Hollywood type of Voodoo, with the doll and the pin needles, no real life, Santeria, Voodoun, spiritual realm, trance like state of mind Voodoo. Talking to the Loa or the spirits of this practice rooted in Africa. I remember my aunt praying to Papa Legba, the gate keeper to the Loa, in order to properly access the spirits and gain help. I had tried all of that, but nothing really dealt with my feelings after being raped in college. Nothing dealt with the abortion I had when I was fresh out of college, after realizing the guy I was dating was not daddy or husband material, and that was not who I wanted to be with, or how I couldn't talk to anyone about it. My best

"Suicidal?" he asked.

"I mean, no, I haven't felt like that in a while, at least I don't think so," I said.

"Start with one thing that is hurting you right now," he probed.

"Weakness. I feel weak."

"What is making you feel weak?"

"My job, this man I met recently, life."

"All right, let's start there"

My session lasted for about forty minutes. It was everything I needed. At least for now. I made it home and lay in bed for about two hours, replaying everything over and over in my mind. I must have called and texted Dean a million times, although I never pressed send or hit the talk icon to actually let the call go through. I really felt like I was going crazy. I knew from experience that I couldn't stay in this mind state, I kept telling myself, "Snap out of it." I tried watching my favorite shows, but I couldn't get my mind to stop thinking about Dean Foster. I drank several glasses of wine and decided that I had to pull myself together. I couldn't let this man consume my every waking hour. I called up my girlfriends Teka and Constance. I needed them to talk some sense into me. Teka Nolan. Our city's high-powered defense attorney. This lady had a way with words, she would convince you that your name was incorrect, and the sky was green if you let her. She lived in an upscale part of town with her choice of men, and was always invited to the latest and greatest political soirees. Her last event was the inauguration dinner for the newly elected mayor of our city. She was the girlfriend who you always sent your email to before sending it to the intended recipients. Dr. Constance Barry as the district's assistant school superintendent who was passionate about making life better for the youth in our schools in grades pre-k-12. She worked hard and played harder, always jet setting across the country. I often lived vicariously through her. Her last romp had her visiting the ancient ruins of the Egyptian pyramids. These two were the ones who I let know some of my issues, although even they didn't know it all.

"Girl, so wait a minute, let me get this shit straight, you went over there damn near butt-ass naked, and he threw your ass out in the morning? You sure you was putting it down right?" Constance said jokingly.

We all laughed. I desperately needed that laughter. Sisters have a way of breaking down barriers, and telling the hard truth. I wondered for a moment, that maybe that's what the issue was, but on the inside, I knew this was going to happen. Black women try to laugh away the pain. They need to give one another a jolt in the arm. Give a reason to be strong, and to move on. No matter how much pain we are in, we have to find a way to deal with it. The world doesn't stop to acknowledge our issues. Heck, outside of culture appropriation the world doesn't stop to acknowledge us at all. There isn't going to be a national conversation about what we go through each and every day, no *Lifetime* special, no council appointment by the president to delve deep into the issues, we just have to deal with it.

"You just have to figure out how you are going to put your game face on and deal with this shit when you get back into work on Monday," Teka added.

'I already contacted the proper personnel, I am taking a few weeks off. I wouldn't be able to deal with seeing him every day right now. Thank God for health insurance!"

"I know, that's right," Constance said. "We all have good insurance, it's time we started using it."

"Are you sure that's what you want to do?" Teka added.

"I know, I thought about going in there and showing him that I was fierce, and he didn't affect me, but the truth is, I could barely stand up straight the morning he put me out of his house, so I know I would be a hot mess, trying to see him."

"Niggas ain't shit," Constance added. "Wait, no let me be clear, that nigga ain't shit, I don't want to lump them all in the same ain't shit category."

We laughed hard at that one.

I could always depend on my girls to cheer me up. As I bid them goodnight, I washed the dishes, cleaned the kitchen, showered and even re-twisted some of my locks. I was watching the latest episode of *Queen Sugar* on Demand, when my text message signal sounded. I knew before looking down who it was.

"If I call will you pick up?"

Ignore.

"Zee, please answer me."

"Zee, I need to talk to you, please. I want to explain."

"I know you see these messages. Is this what you want, you want to throw me away like everyone else? I am not worth fighting for?"

Damn it! Why was he doing this to me? When I told Dr. Fritz that I was feeling weak, it was because of this man. He was my weakness. I hadn't felt this vulnerable in a long time. I kept wrestling with my options in my head. Should I respond via text and tell his ass to go fuck himself? Should I forgive him? Should I try to figure out what he means by throwing him away like everyone else? Why couldn't I shake this man? You would think that I had dated him for years the way I was acting, the way he had a hold on me. What was it about me that kept attracting, low lives the likes of Dean Foster? I mean who does what he did this morning? Take me to such heights of ecstasy and then just treat me like trash afterward. How do I forgive something like that? I tried to give myself the best "sister be strong" pep talk, with so many valid points, but the truth was, this man had the key to my heart or the knife and was just twisting away, or maybe I was doing it to myself. A knife does not know who its master is.

I couldn't help myself. I texted back.

"Why are you doing this?" I replied.

"I can explain. Just give me a chance to see you, to talk to you," he texted back immediately.

"No. I can't. This isn't fair, this isn't what I signed up for."

"What did you sign up for? A fairytale? Shit, Zee, that's not how it works."

"Maybe I did sign up for a fairytale, but you are my nightmare, Dean Foster, not my knight in shining armor."

"Like I said, that's not how it works, you black women have your head so far up your asses, thinking shit really happens like that!"

"Oh, so the way it works is to kick me out of your house, after what we shared! To treat me like some common street whore, it that how it works? Is that the type of relationship we black women should aspire to have?"

"It might be, I can't speak for anybody else, I can only take responsibility for my actions."

"So now you want to be the responsible one, are you kidding me?"

"I need to see you, or talk to you over the phone, I'm not going to keep going back and forth with you via text."

"You don't get to call the shots, you don't get to dictate the rules."

"Yes, I do. I will be there in twenty minutes."

This motherfucker right here.

Why didn't I text back and let him know that if he tried coming over, I would have the police ready to meet him, or better yet, I could just not answer when he comes to my door? I knew that was all wishful thinking. He would come over, and my dumb ass will let him in.

We sat across from each other silently for what seemed like forever and a day. Each of us solemn, in our own state of mind, afraid of throwing the first grenade that would ignite a war. In my mind, I was torn between loving this man, wanting this man, and hating his very existence. What's worse is, it was taking a toll on me mentally. I had worked hard over the years to understand my illness, although few even knew that I suffered from bouts of depression. I didn't want to be labeled as crazy or even worse, weak. I had learned that depression manifests itself in many ways, at times it could be the reason for my anxiety, my weight fluctuations, and my impulsivity. Then there were the times, when loneliness consumed me. That is why it was hard to stay in a committed relationship for very long. Naturally, men I dated just assumed I was too needy, or too demanding, unstable, or just crazy. I never shared my condition with anyone, and I didn't have any plans to do so in the near future.

"I don't know where to start," Dean began, "so I am just going to lay all my cards on the table, and you can do with it what you want.

"I didn't grow up with my parents, they were both heavy drug users and weren't interested in raising me or my siblings. I grew up with an aunt and uncle who I wouldn't care if they dropped dead today. They treated me like shit, and both abused me when I was younger. If it wasn't for my eighth grade teacher who took notice of me and my potential, I might still be back home, maybe on drugs, locked up or at a dead end job. I was offered a full ride to a military school, for high school. From there I went on to college. I suffer from Residual Schizophrenia. When I take my medication, I am fine. I can't stand liars, I don't get into long relationships, because when I have tried, the women can't handle what I bring to the table. That's it. That's all."

My mind was spinning. He just said a mouthful, and acted like he was reading the teleprompter as the 11:00 news anchor on the local news. Did he just say he suffers from Schizophrenia? What in the world?"

"Whoa, wait…I…," was all I managed to get out.

"Look, Zee, I know it's a lot to take in."

You think?

"I am not asking you to marry me tomorrow, I'm just asking that you give us a chance." "I am not perfect, far from it, but I am willing to see where this goes."

"Dean…I mean, I don't know what to say. I have so many questions."

"I'm not a lab experiment, you don't get to dissect me and shit, you want to know the details of the abuse, the illness?"

"Yes," I countered. Why was he acting like he just told me he likes to ski, this could be a deal breaker. I thought I had issues, but damn. I can hardly keep my shit together, and now what? Was I expected to jump head first into a relationship with a man who clearly had issues far beyond my scope of understanding?

"Zee, I mean, I don't know what else you want me to say. I can't go into details right now, but maybe in time. Will you be around? If not just let me know now. I told you before I don't have time for games."

Here is your chance, Zee, I thought. He is giving you a clean break. Take it.

"I am here. I want to help you get through this."

"See, this is why I don't share my shit! I am not a fucking charity case, Zee! I don't need your help. I need you. I need you in my life, by my side, that's what I need."

"Okay. I didn't mean to upset you."

"You didn't, I mean, I'm not upset, it's just people look at me differently when I share my past or my condition with them."

"How many people have you told?"

"Not many. Definitely not anyone at the job. I only shared it with one other woman I dated, after dating her for a while, and as soon as I told her, she just used it against me, to try to sabotage our relationship. She eventually left, and the rest, as they say is history."

I got up and walked over to where he was sitting and sat next to him. At this moment, I just wanted to hold him. I could tell it took everything he had to share with me what he did. From what I knew about his condition, it could be responsible for tremendous mood swings, which would explain his behavior the other morning. I wanted to fix it. Another burden of the black woman, or maybe women in general, always thinking we can fix what we believe to be wrong with our men. When will we learn? I placed my hand on his face, and rubbed his cheek through his beard. He pulled away.

"Zee, I don't need you to feel sorry for me. Don't treat me differently, I am a big boy, I can handle my issues. What I can't handle is someone not being up front with me. Is there anything, anything at all that you want to tell me?"

Go ahead, let him know your issues, and see if he doesn't go running through the door, part of my mind said, the other part screamed, tell him, he will stay, like you are staying for him.

I couldn't risk it.

"What do you mean is there something I need to tell you?" I said defensively.

"I mean, a beautiful woman such as yourself, I find it hard to believe that you aren't already involved with someone."

Whew! Is that all he thought?

"What? No, I am not seeing anyone else," I asserted.

"You sure?" he asked. "So this thing that we shared, is not part of some diabolical plan you have to ruin my career?"

"What? Plan? No, that's ridiculous."

"So, there is no one else?" he asked again.

"Yes," I assured him again. Technically I wasn't lying to him. I just wasn't ready to tell him everything about me. He should have been my example of bravery, of courage despite the fear of failure, but I just couldn't bring myself to share with him all of my demons. Besides, I was receiving help for my depression, I took my meds regularly, it wasn't like, I was dealing with issues like him. Clearly his issues were far worse, far more painful. My condition was manageable. What he didn't know wouldn't hurt him, I finally convinced myself.

I reached for him again. This time he didn't pull away. He kissed my hand as it lay on his face. He kissed each finger. He kissed my arm, he pulled me close. There wasn't the tenderness in his touch like the first time. It was as if he had to show me he was still a man, despite what he shared and I let him. We slid down to the floor. I didn't waste any time getting undressed. I needed him now more than ever. I wanted to please him in every way I knew how. He laid, more like pushed, my back on the floor and placed his hand around my neck. There was no doubt that I loved this man.

It is scary how that works. We are so inundated with how love is supposed to unfold. So many people define the strength of the relationship by the length of their relationship, but nothing could be further from the truth. We are taught that two people are supposed to meet, have great dates and take long walks in the park, holding hands and unveiling their souls to each other at just the right moment, but in reality, love is beautifully messy. It happens in an instant for some people, and that moment has me caught up.

Our hands interlocked over my head, while he kissed me passionately on my neck, his lips wet with desire. He stopped and stared at me for a while, it was as if he was trying to gauge whether or not he had made a mistake in sharing his secret with me. I wanted to assure him that it was not.

"I love you, Dean Foster."

"Hmm," he moaned. "Tell me again."

"I love you, Dean Foster."

I was already wet when he entered me. As he pumped in and out, his moans, made me somewhat delusional, he placed my legs on his shoulders and kissed my inner thighs, while his fingers, first one, then several, gave me the best pleasure between my legs. I trembled. I closed my eyes, overcome with the intimacy.

"Open your eyes. I want you to experience every moment with me."

Feeling him inside me felt so good. I needed some assurance myself.

"How do I feel?"

"You feel like mine," he said. "And it better stay that way. You better always feel like this."

We ended up in the 69 position. The feeling was exhilarating. His hands holding my hips and my ass just right while he went to town on my lovebox. I did the same for him. I worked that pole, as if I was trying to extract his soul. I licked every inch and acted as if his manhood was my favorite piece of candy. I could barely keep up with all his energy, he made me feel like I was on a natural high. My knees gave out on me and I buckled several times from the sheer enjoyment I was experiencing. He slapped my ass several times, and with each slap, the sting felt like the best mixture of pleasure and pain. That is what our relationship had been so far. A combination of my highest of highs and my lowest of lows.

After we explored every inch of each other's bodies, I got on top. His hands switching from my hips to encourage me to ride harder and faster and my breast, touching, pinching, kissing, caressing and sucking them had me going crazy. I came at least three times, each time trying my best to wait until he allowed me to do so. It was another way he could exhibit control, but I didn't mind it. I didn't mind it at all.

$\mathcal{D}ean$

I knew it was a risk, but I didn't mind. I didn't mind it at all. I wanted this woman to know me, and I knew that if I had any shot of having a real and honest relationship with her, I had to let her know. I couldn't keep my condition a secret. I wanted to build something with her, and I knew that foundation could not be built upon lies. As we lay there, after an hour of lovemaking, my arm around her, stroking her shoulder and arm with my hand, I knew she wasn't asleep. I knew she wanted to ask me a million questions, but didn't know how to approach it, so I helped her out.

"What do you want to know, Zee?"

"What?

"C'mon, Zee, don't do that, I know you are thinking about it, just tell me what you want to know, and I will try my best to answer."

"You said your aunt and uncle abused you."

"What's the question, Zee?"

"I mean, how did they abuse you?"

"I mean abuse is abuse, I don't know if you need to know all the details, but in a nutshell, they both were high most of the time, and when they couldn't get high, they took it out on me. That could be hitting me, depriving me of food, because they spent the money they did get on drugs, and my aunt sexually abused me."

"Why do you describe such horrible things so mundanely? I mean, you say it like it doesn't bother you."

"It wasn't always that way, Zee, but I can't cry about it either. What's done is done, it doesn't do me any good to dwell on it. It happened a long time ago. They had demons that they didn't know how to deal with, so I learned to develop a tough skin. No one in this world is going to feel sorry for a black man. Anything else?"

"Okay, so your condition, when were you diagnosed?"

"A few years ago. I had episodes where I would wake up and realize that I had slept in the same position all night, or that people were telling me that I showed no emotion or improper emotion when I spoke to them or during inappropriate times. In other words I had a flat effect that was abnormal. My speech became really disorganized, and it was very difficult for me to think clearly, which of course affected my ability to behave rationally. And as you can imagine this led to some destructive behaviors on my part."

"But that sounds like many people I know."

"It may, residual schizophrenia is one of the subtypes of schizophrenia. Many people have never heard of it. Most people only hear of paranoid schizophrenia. That's where people experience extreme episodes of hallucinations or delusions."

"Do you experience those too?" she asked.

"Not in a very long time. The thing about my condition is I can go long periods of time without experiencing any of the symptoms. This period is called waning. As long as I take my medication and go to my psycho-therapy sessions, I can function like any other normal human being."

I can feel her body tense up.

"Zee, you don't have to be afraid of me. I am not going to hurt you. Most people who are diagnosed with any of the five types of schizophrenia are more likely to harm themselves than others. The suicide rate is very high for those who do not seek or maintain medical treatment."

"Is there anything I can do to make sure that you…"

Chapter 4

Nobody but My Baby
Zee

I got up in the middle of the night and made sure not to disturb Dean Foster, as I left the bedroom and made my way to the kitchen. I pulled my laptop out and immediately Google searched "Residual Schizophrenia." I had never heard of it before tonight. I know Dean did his best to try to explain the condition to me, but I needed more information. I needed to know exactly what I was dealing with. As I skimmed through the endless search results, it wasn't missed on me that he didn't say I love you back earlier, but I knew that would be a big step for him, one that he may not be ready to take right now. I would have to wrestle with those thoughts at a later time.

"What are you doing?"

I nearly jumped out of my seat.

"Oh my God, Dean, you scared the shit out of me! Why did you sneak up on me like that?"

"I wasn't sneaking. Answer the question."

Think fast, Zee. Should I tell him the truth, or play it off?

"I was researching your condition."

"Why?" he demanded.

"I wanted to learn more about it."

"Why not just ask me?"

"You were sleeping, I didn't want to disturb you."

"Don't lie to me, Zee."

"I am not lying."

"If you want to know something about me, ask me, ain't shit you can find out about me on the internet that I can't tell you myself."

"I just wanted to learn more about you"

"And so you figured the best way to do that was to look it up on Google?"

"It's not like that."

"Did you find what you were looking for?"

"I started to. I mean I didn't get a chance to read through everything that came up when I searched your…your condition."

"I asked you earlier to give us a fair chance. Shit like this makes me think that you may not be ready to do that."

"Dean, I am not trying to be unfair, I just wanted to take some time and learn about your condition on my own terms. That's all. I hardly see that as not being fair."

"How about we agree to disagree? Can you come back to bed now?"

It was a question, but it really didn't offer me a real choice.

"Of course."

I logged off and closed my laptop and made my way to my man. The last thing I wanted to do was make him feel like I was already trying to undermine our relationship.

When the morning finally rolled around, I got up and made a breakfast fit for a king. Eggs, turkey bacon for me and vegan bacon for Dean, pancakes, hash browns, grits, and French toast. I had coffee and orange juice on the table as well. As we sat across from one another, I can clearly hear our forks hitting our plates. The sound was deafening, or maybe I was just in tune to my surroundings. I felt like ever since last night, I was hyper sensitive. I didn't want to act like I was trying to catch everything he did and associate his behavior with his condition, but I couldn't help it. He didn't want me researching the thing, but I felt like if I kept asking him questions he would be upset about that too. I hated walking on eggshells.

"So when do you think you are going to come back to work?" he asked.

"Umm, I don't know, I was granted leave for a few weeks."

"Oh, yeah, based on what?"

Shit. If I tell him the real reason, my depression, then he will know that I wasn't up front with him last night when he asked was there anything about me that I wanted to share. I will seem like the worst person on earth. I couldn't come clean now. I knew he would try to ask around and dig up some information from human resources, but my medical condition is confidential, and they are not allowed to share it with anyone, not even my immediate supervisors.

"Umm, well, I just told them I suffered from some really bad migraines."

"Do you?"

"What do you mean?"

"I mean, do you really suffer from migraines or did you just find a doctor to vouch for you so you can take off?"

"A bit of both."

"How is it a bit of both?"

"I mean, I have had migraines in the past that were so debilitating, that I have had to take a few days off from work."

"A few days is different from a few weeks. You had to take FMLA. You gaming the system?"

"To tell you the truth, I just needed some time away from you."

"From me?" He sounded surprised.

'Yes, I mean when I left your house that morning you kicked me out, I just knew it would be awhile before I could collect my bearings enough to deal with you on a daily basis. I was humiliated, and really hurt."

"How about now?"

"Wait, let's not just skim over that part, you are not going to address that morning first?"

"No."

"Really? You don't think you owe me an apology?"

"I owe you an explanation, I gave that to you. I don't owe you an apology."

"Oh, so your behavior that morning is due to your condition? Is that what we are doing now?"

"We are not talking about my condition this morning. We are talking about you. I just need to know when you plan to come back to work. If you are gaming the system, you need to stop, that's dishonest and I hate liars."

"I'll think about it," I said.

'I expect to see you at work by the end of the week." Another command. This man was so controlling.

I let it go. I could have pushed more, maybe spoken up and let him know that he wasn't going to determine my return date, but I knew he had a thing about honesty, and people lying to him and I guess he felt like this was being dishonest.

"Why are you so adamant about not riding with men you don't know?'

That statement caught me completely off guard. This nigga was 20/20 questions this morning. I should have prepared some charts, data and graphs.

"What are you talking about?"

"Why do you always do that?"

"Do what?"

"Avoid answering a question you clearly heard the first time, by answering it with a question, or asking for clarity. It's like you are trying to avoid the question or trying to buy time to answer the question. It can be annoying."

Damn, this man was on point. How is he able to see right through me? I am not going to able to hide much from him. I have to be on my toes.

"I think you read too much into things. Do we have to do this right now? It's a nice fall day. Can we do something outside of the house maybe?"

"This is classic avoidance."

"Is it?"

"I don't know, but it sounded good." He laughed.

Good, I thought, that meant he wasn't going to press the issue, at least for now. I liked seeing the lighter side of him. I felt like the room was getting too serious.

We showered, got dressed and headed out. We went to a new art gallery that had just opened up downtown. I had read about it in a blog by a sister named Tamia Reynolds: "Top 10 Cultural Things to Do while in Washington, D.C., While Still Supporting Black-Owned Businesses."

I commented and admired the paintings on the wall that were part of an exhibit and the ones that were for sale. I even bought a piece that depicted a picture of Emitt Till and Trayvon Martin. I was admiring the other similar pieces that hung beautifully on the white walls, while Dean was on the other side of the gallery checking out the sculptures and speaking to other patrons doing the same.

"I see you are interested in these types of pieces," a voice said, that got me out of my own thoughts.

I turned around and saw a very distinguished, fine-looking gentleman in a clearly tailor-made suit standing beside me. He was tall and lean, but well built. He was clean shaven with salt and pepper hair that was cut perfectly. His brown skin was flawless, and his smile held two dimples that nearly sucked me in when he spoke.

"Yes. I find pieces that connect our past to our present, no matter how disturbing or tragic, very interesting," I said.

"Oh, yeah? Please elaborate," he said.

"I mean, it's just crazy how more than fifty years after the murder of Emitt Till we are still dealing with the same issues. Our children are still being murdered because of the color of their skin, and no one is held accountable."

"I feel you. Many thought that after we elected Barack Obama, we were living in a post-racial society, and nothing could be further from the truth."

"Exactly! I am so tired of marching, and singing we shall overcome, while our men, women and children are murdered in the streets every day."

"Oh, but wait, don't you know that All Lives Matter?" He laughed.

"Oh, please don't even get me started on that bullshit!"

"I share those sentiments. Excuse my manners, my name is Quincy Boroughs."

"Hi, nice to meet you, I'm Zenia Warren, but most people just call me Zee."

"What do I have to do to not be most people?"

All I could do was blush.

"Wait a minute, Quincy Boroughs? Aren't you the curator of this establishment?"

"Well, yes, yes, I am." He laughed. "What gave me away?"

"Well, it took me a minute, but your name is on the marque!"

"Yeah, I guess that would do it."

We both laughed.

"So I am always pleased when I have a beautiful woman such as yourself visit my gallery. How do I ensure that I keep it that way?"

Was this man flirting with me? He was coming on strong. I looked over across the room, and I can tell that Dean had spotted my new found admirer, but he continued to make small talk with the group he was conversing with.

"Well, it may be a good idea to host an event here, you know, maybe a book talk, or signing, an up and coming artist and his/her pieces, maybe even a party or cocktail hour for business professionals."

"See, I knew there was a reason that I was drawn to you. I am actually looking for a marketing or PR person."

"No, I don't actually have any experience doing that type of stuff."

"Experience is overrated. I mean for God's sake, this country elected Donald Trump president. Unless you are a medical doctor, anything can be learned by just actually doing the task."

"I appreciate your vote of confidence," I said.

"Well, look, just think about it, I am always looking to meet new people and have them share ideas about how to make this place a success, so here is my card."

He handed me his card and took extra care to lightly squeeze my hand as I took the card from him.

"Do you have a card or a number where I can reach you?" he asked.

Why does it always happen like this? Anytime you begin to develop serious feelings about someone, or start dating exclusively, it seems like men just come out of the woodwork, willing to wine and dine you, offer you jobs and shit! What harm would it do to at least entertain the idea of working with this fine man, even if the idea never came to fruition?

"Hey, babe, you good?" Dean interrupted, before I was able to answer Mr. Boroughs. I was so wrapped up in Mr. Curator, I didn't even notice Dean had made his way over to me.

"Um, yes, I'm fine. Dean, I would like for you to meet Quincy Boroughs, the curator."

They shook hands and exchanged small talk. Dean made it a point to place his hand on my lower back while he spoke to Quincy. Almost as if he was marking his territory. I wasn't quite sure how I felt about it.

Once they were done, and Quincy walked away, Dean removed his hand. How convenient.

"What were the two of you talking about?"

"Mostly just about the piece that I purchased."

"That's it?"

"What do you mean?"

"I mean was that all the conversation was about, he didn't try to holler at you?"

"Where is this nonsense coming from? I am allowed to talk to people of the opposite sex, you know."

"Why are you getting so defensive?"

"Because I feel like you are trying to interrogate me for having a conversation."

"Let's just drop it."

"Let's," I replied, my response full of attitude. This was becoming suffocating. I mean I truly did love this man, but I was starting to regret the fact that he shared so much of himself with me. Maybe, we would be better off, if I didn't know. This just validated the reason why I couldn't share my depression episodes with Dean. My every thought of him was now laced in the reality he shared. I could not have him doing the same toward me.

After we left the art gallery, we ate lunch at the Cheesecake Factory, grabbed a few groceries, and then headed back to my home. Once there, we watched a movie, ate dinner and I took a nap. The day had worn me out, but I was also toying with the idea of actually calling Mr. Curator, and seeing if he was serious about maybe me helping him with marketing his establishment. As I lay in bed daydreaming and feigning sleep, I could hear Dean in the living room watching a basketball game. He was rooting for his hometown team, the New York Knicks. God only knows you have to be a true fan to root for a team that consistently disappoints. After a while, Dean came to my bedroom doorway. The room was dark, but I could feel him standing there staring at me. I must admit, I was little scared. What was he thinking? I know he told me that I shouldn't be afraid of him, but his behavior earlier today at breakfast, last night when he got upset about me researching his condition, even his behavior at the gallery, just had me over thinking everything.

"Stop acting like you're sleeping," he said as he sat at the foot of the bed.

"I'm not," I replied. "I actually don't feel too hot."

"What's wrong, babe? I noticed you hardly touched your food today at lunch and barely ate your dinner. Maybe you are coming down with a 24-hour bug or something."

"I know, I guess my eyes were bigger than my stomach." I smiled.

"Okay, well, is there anything I can do to make you feel more comfortable?"

"No, I probably just need to lie down for a while, it's been a long day."

"All right, well, after the game, I am going to go ahead and head home, I have some things I need to complete for tomorrow. I'll be sure to call you, okay?"

"Okay. I'd like that."

He got up and walked to the head of the bed, leaned down and planted a kiss on my lips. After about an hour, I could hear him make his way out the front door. After being asleep for a while I suddenly had the urge to get up and go to the bathroom. It felt like I had to throw up, but couldn't. I hated that feeling. On my way back to my bed I grabbed my phone off the dresser and saw that I had a few missed calls from Dr. Constance Barry, Dean and an unknown number. I figured I would get some more sleep and return the calls in the morning.

The next three weeks went by uneventfully. I tied up some loose ends and prepared myself to report back to work this morning. I chose Friday, the last day of the week, because it would be a good test run on how the rest of the semester would unfold and if it didn't go well, at least I would have the weekend to regroup and recover. It seemed like the weeks had flown by. I couldn't believe we were already heading into the tail end of the year. My relationship with Dean was going as well as could be expected. I managed to do some more research on my own on his condition, despite his objections. I learned that individuals with residual-type schizophrenia may exhibit an array of symptoms during the active phase. Although this is considered one of the five main subtypes of schizophrenia, there's really no predictable set of symptoms—it varies depending on the person. Certain individuals with residual-type may experience an isolated schizophrenic episode or two, but may have gone months without symptoms. It was obvious that Dean was in this phase, and I was thankful.

We had spent quite of bit of time with one another over the last few weeks. He always made sure he came to see me after work. I could always hear his car pulling up my long driveway. He would take me out to lunch somedays when he wasn't too busy. It seemed that we ate at every soul vegan, urban, and fancy restaurant the city had to offer. We took walks around downtown, and went to open houses of newly renovated brownstones in the hood. We loved to see how the gentrification movement, had transformed these once dilapidated homes into jaw dropping spaces. We visited the MLK memorial and talked for hours about the African-American History Museum that had just opened up not too long ago. I enjoyed showing him my city. One weekend we drove to his hometown of NYC, and stayed in Manhattan. It was amazing. He was definitely in his element. He made sure to take me to all the popular venues, and some that only true New Yorkers knew about. We had the best food, and even caught an off-Broadway play. This was a bonafide relationship. I was so glad that I had given him a chance, and I could tell that he was grateful I did too. But more importantly, I was so happy that he had given me a chance. My relationships never seem to last past lust and infatuation. They always seem to fade off into the sunset. I was proud of myself for having the courage to open up, just a little. I liked it here, in this world of togetherness. He made not have verbally apologized for the night he degraded me, but his actions were like he was saying sorry over and over again. I accepted his way of reconciling the situation and making me feel whole, and loved.

After a long hiatus, I walked onto campus and into the office I shared with my colleagues and was greeted by several of my co-workers. They all welcomed me back with open arms and it felt nice to have them be so warm toward me. We talked about all the latest gossip in and around the office, my students, and the pile of work I had to tackle before the semester was over. I was also greeted with enthusiasm by most of my students. They all wanted to know about my wellbeing, before I was able to even go into the heart of any of my lectures. I must admit, I missed teaching and helping these students become better writers and critical thinkers, and it was heartwarming to know that I had made a small impact on their lives. The day wouldn't be complete, however, until I was able to see Dean Foster. I waited until just the right moment, when my office space that I shared with several other professors was not so crowded, before placing a call to his office.

"Hey, Dean Foster."

"Hey, beautiful, how are you? How is your day going so far?"

I loved how tender he could be.

"I can't complain, as a matter of fact, it's almost like I never left. My students, and everyone in the department has treated me so nicely."

"You were missed," he reassured me.

"Did you miss me?" I asked.

"When are you going to come see me?" he asked.

"This is classic avoidance."

We both laughed at the inside joke.

"Let me see you after your last class," he asserted.

"Of course."

As I made my way to my last class, notes in tow, I was eager to get it over and done with. On my way to the classroom, I suddenly felt my stomach in my throat. I had to find relief fast. I made my way to the nearest bathroom and upchucked the little bit of lunch that I had earlier that afternoon. I rinsed my mouth out and washed my face. As I stared at my reflection in the mirror, I thought about the last time I had my monthly friend and the night I wasn't feeling well, when Dean came over. I realized that I was already a week late. This could be the reason why I was feeling so bad over the last few days. Dean and I didn't use protection, so it didn't take a rocket scientist to surmise that I could very well be pregnant. I had a wide mix of emotions. I can't say that I was trying not to get pregnant, because we were not taking any precautions to avoid it, but at the same time, I was in tune with my body and thought I knew when I was ovulating, and the peak time for me to get pregnant, but apparently there are exceptions. I couldn't take too long to process all the thoughts racing through my mind in the bathroom, I had a class to teach.

I entered my class, a few minutes before students were scheduled to arrive to set up my technology. I had the Prezi all set, and my handouts ready to pass out to the class. This evening's topic was comparing and contrasting the essays in the book *In Search of Our Mother's Gardens* by Alice Walker and Sister Outsider, *Essays and Speeches* by Audre Lourde. I was hoping to inspire and give an exemplary outline of writing as students prepared to write their own compelling essays. I was writing key components of an effective essay on chart paper, when several students started piling in. After a few minutes, I turned around to begin my lesson. I got the shock of my life as Mr. Curator was sitting in the back row. How in the world did Quincy Boroughs end up here? I tried to keep my cool and recall the last few days. I remember receiving a call from an unknown number the night I wasn't feeling well.

When I called the number back in the morning it was Mr. Boroughs. We talked for about an hour, picking up right where we left off in the gallery. I asked him how he got my number and he swore on his great-grandmother's grave that I had given it to him. I didn't remember doing so, but nevertheless, I must have. How else would he have gotten my number? I could hardly get my lecture started with the man staring at me from the back of the room. The hour-and-a-half class seemed to drag on. He sat quietly, just eying me the entire time. This wasn't high school, so the other students in the classroom, didn't pay any particular attention to him. They must have just figured he was just joining the class, or perhaps sitting in for a session. Once the class wrapped up, Mr. Curator made his way to where I was standing behind the podium, as I was gathering my things.

He feigned a hand clap gesture. "That was a wonderful class. You got me thinking I should have paid more attention in my creative writing classes during college."

"Oh, really?" was all I could manage to say.

"I certainly don't remember many of my professors looking like you. Thank you for inviting me."

"What? Wait, I invited you here?" I said.

I didn't mean to say it out loud, but that was exactly what I was thinking. I had little memory of even having a conversation with Mr. Boroughs outside of the gallery, let alone inviting him to come to one of my classes. Why would I do that, and risk Dean Foster seeing him? It didn't make any sense.

"Oh, you are trying to be funny, huh?" he said with those dimples flashing.

"No, of course not," I lied. "Of course I remember, I just thought I asked you to come to another class, that's all."

"So, you found it interesting?" I tried to sound convincing.

"No. I am pretty sure, you told me to come check you out during tonight's class. He wouldn't let me off the hook that easily. So, are we still up for coffee or don't you remember that either?"

"No, of course I do," I lied again. "It's just that I am feeling a bit under the weather, do you mind if we take a raincheck?" I wasn't lying when I said I was feeling out of sorts. Not just physically, but with this latest episode, mentally as well. This whole thing just seemed like some type of misunderstanding.

"As a matter of fact, I do mind," he responded bluntly, "but it looks like I can't do anything about it. If the lady isn't feeling well, what type of man would I be, to keep you from getting better?" He moved closer to me and we were now standing inches apart. This man was taking up all the air in the room, I felt like I was going to pass out.

I could still hear several students in the hallway, discussing the class, and I could hear the professor across the hall, wrapping up his lecture. The soles of the feet, the conversations, the laughter, the sound of roller bags moving across the hallway floor all sounded like a cacophony in B minor. I needed some reprise from the discord. I needed to get out of here immediately.

"So," Quincy chimed in.

Kiss on the neck.

"I."

Kiss on the other side of my neck.

"Will."

Kiss on the lips.

"Call you later."

Another kiss on the lips.

I damned near passed out on the floor.

"Okay. I will speak to you tomorrow," was all I could muster up to say.

Mr. Boroughs finally left after a few more minutes of casual conversation. Now I had to collect my bearings and go see Dean as promised. Dean Foster was so in tune with me, I was sure he was going to be able to know everything that just transpired in this room. He would probably string me along, just to see if I was telling the truth. The mere fact that I couldn't remember inviting Quincy to my workplace scared the living daylights out of me. How much more had I shared with this man? Perhaps the medication I took the night I talked with him over the phone had clouded my memory to the point where I didn't remember any details at all. What other plans did I conjure up with Mr. Boroughs that I wasn't aware of? Was this the first time we've seen each other since the gallery? Had we been intimate? It was obvious to me that we must have had more than one conversation. I could only imagine what I shared with that man over the phone. I would have to fix it, and fix it fast. I had clearly given him the impression that we had a shot at something. A man isn't just going to plant kisses on your neck if you don't give him some type of green light.

I finished packing my things, went to the bathroom and splashed some cold water on my face. I ate two peppermints and was finally knocking at the door of the man I loved.

"Heyyyy," I said in a sing-song voice as he beckoned me in.

"I see you finally made it," he said, his hand over the receiver of the phone. He motioned for me to come toward him, and I obliged.

I sat on his lap, as he wrapped up his phone call.

"Great, President Fleischman, I look forward to meeting with you on Monday," I heard him say. His smile was from ear to ear.

The way he hung up the phone, I could tell he was on cloud nine.

"Sounds like somebody has got some good news."

"I hope so. It may be nothing, but you know I am trying to make moves, and this meeting could be helping me cement some things in place."

"That's my man! You better go, boy!" I said in my best Gina Waters voice.

He smiled, and pulled me close. His hands were wrapped around my waist, and he was rubbing my ass while simultaneously kissing me, making his way down my breast.

"Baby, what are you doing?" I asked.

"What?" he asked. "C'mon, don't try to act shy now. There is nothing shy about you." There was something about the way he said that last phrase, as if he was insinuating something about my character.

I brushed it off. Maybe I was reading too much into things, overanalyzing every comment.

"What if someone walks in?" I worried.

"Then lock the door."

"C'mon, babe, we can pick this back up at my house, or yours."

"Nah, we can pick it up and finish it right here, lock the door."

His tone was unfamiliar; it was a command, not a suggestion. I didn't feel comfortable sleeping with him in the office. We had made love in public spaces before, in my car and his, in the restroom of a restaurant. It wasn't a novel idea. Each time we did, I felt like it was a decision we were making together, to get a thrill. This time didn't feel the same, I didn't want to be intimate with him here, but it was like I didn't have a voice.

He stood up, unzipped his pants and sat back down on his chair as I made my way to the door and locked it. When I walked back over to him, he was already rock hard. He cleared some papers off his desk and motioned for me to stand in front of him. I did.

"Take your clothes off." Command.

I started to undress, pulling my skirt down, and un-buttoning my blouse.

"Slow down, not so fast," he said, while he plea-sured himself.

I blushed, I didn't know how to perform a strip tease, but tried my best to imitate what I saw in movies, saw in strip clubs back in the day, or heard my friends say about the show they had put on for their significant others.

"Look at me," he said.

He reached for me and rubbed my arms, belly and thighs. It was almost like he was looking at me for the first time.

"Putting on a little weight, I see."

My goodness! Nothing got past him, I thought.

Maybe now would be a good time to let him know about my vomiting experience earlier and what it could mean for the both of us. I wanted to change the mood, but I decided against it.

He stood tall and picked me up and placed me on the desk. He held my locks in his hands and rubbed my back for a moment before placing both hands underneath my butt, positioning himself to give me the ultimate pleasure. In what seemed like a second, He quickly removed his hands from underneath me and grabbed me by the neck. His grip was cold and his fingers were digging into my skin. I was in shock. I didn't understand what was happening. It felt like I was in a dream, more like a nightmare wanting desperately to wake up. His eyes, looming, seemed dark all of a sudden, like he was overcome with rage. He grabbed me by my hair and dragged me off the desk, causing me to fall on the floor. I didn't know what to do, I could hardly get my thoughts together, before the blow of his fist caught me in the back of my head. By now, all I could do was try to scream, but his hands grabbed me by my locks again, pulled me up so quickly that I could see the room spinning and pinned me against the wall with his free hand once again around my neck.

"You fucking that nigga?" he said through clenched teeth. "Huh? You fucking that nigga?"

I wanted to answer him, but his chokehold on me made it impossible to speak. I could feel myself lifting off of the ground, at first I thought I was having an outer body experience, maybe this wasn't really happening, but soon realized it was him lifting me off of the ground by my neck.

"I...ca...can't...brea...breathe," was all I could manage to let escape from my lips.

He put me down and I tried to grab all of the air in the room, I felt like my eyes were bulging out of their sockets, my head was throbbing, my neck stung from the grip he had on me, and my whole body ached from being tossed on the floor, but I needed to get out. I would not repeat what I did in college, and just take what was being done to me. I needed to fight. I gathered all the strength I had and attempted to run toward the door, but my feet felt like led boots caught in quick sand that did not allow me to get far. He pulled me back by my hair and slapped me so hard, my head came crashing down on the floor for a second time.

"Dean, please, let me explain. It's not what you think," I managed to say through bated breath.

"Oh, it's not what I think, huh? Well, why don't you tell me what I'm thinking, since you seem to know it all? You gonna sit up here and act like you just didn't have this nigga in your classroom, with his hands all over you, kissing all over you, holding you, and to top it off, doing the shit at of all places, right here! You got a lot of goddamn nerve, you know that. You couldn't even be discreet about it. What were you trying to do?

Then to top it off, your ass, gonna come in here and try to get with me after doing god knows what else with him or to him! That's some foul shit, Zee. I pegged you for a lot of things, but a basic whore wasn't one of them."

"Please," I said through loud sobs. I couldn't let him think that his version of what he saw was the case.

"Shut the fuck up. I don't want to hear shit you got to say. You understand me?"

He stood over me, unrecognizable, but I knew him. I wondered for a brief moment if this was the man I had come to love, respect and admire, or was it another version of himself, the one where his illness took over. I knew I was making excuses for his behavior, but I couldn't help to still see the human side of him, even while he was acting like a monster.

I could taste the blood in my mouth, and swallowed my saliva, to try to quench the pain. I had been here before. I wanted to explain, but even I didn't know what to say to make the situation better. All I could do was brace myself for what was coming. I lay still, completely naked, too afraid to move for fear of another blow to the head.

"I'm sorry, Dean, please," I pleaded again.

"I see you like to beg, huh?"

He walked over by his desk and grabbed my clothes and walked out. The look he gave me before walking out was one of disgust and contempt. What was I going to do now? I was completely naked in his office, on the floor. I knew that by this time most students and faculty were gone for the day. The cleaning crew would be here in a few hours. I thought about running out in the hallway screaming and calling for the authorities, but a familiar voice from my past stopped me in my tracks. The voice held onto me until my thoughts became inaction. I was paralyzed by the sophomore girl in college I once was, I wanted to be my own hero, and rewrite the narrative of my inability to stand up for myself, but I was a long song away from riding the melodic waves of self-love. Who am I? Who would believe me? At this point, I could only think about the life that was most likely growing inside of me. No one else mattered. Nobody but my baby.

Chapter 5

Here Comes the Pain Again
Zee

I sat in a corner for what seemed like forever. I was crying uncontrollably. What made me think that I could just act as if my encounter with Quincy Boroughs never happened? How did I think I was going to sweep that under the rug? I am not sure how he found out, and frankly it didn't matter now. I just knew that this would surely be the end of our relationship. I was fairly certain, that Dean would not forgive my transgression. At this point, my biggest obstacle was getting out of this office. I contemplated just walking out again, but didn't want to risk the embarrassment. All of the questions that would arise, and or course the scrutiny that would become of Dean's life. We had already violated the college's Code of Personal Conduct Code by being together. I didn't want to ruin my chances of ever working in this field again. I felt like I owed it to him to not put him through any more than I already did. I sat crouched in the corner of his office, waiting and hoping that he would return with my clothes and just allow me to leave. I made up my mind that I would just leave him alone afterward; he wouldn't have to worry about me disrupting his life any further. Thank God his office had its own bathroom. I gathered enough strength to just go in there and wait until he returned, that way if the cleaning crew did come in, I would be locked away in the bathroom, and just tell them I was working late on a project with Dr. Foster. Three hours passed by and still nothing. I thought about calling him, but was too afraid. By the fourth hour, I figured, I would have to put those fears aside. I called, but he did not answer. After multiple attempts, I just gave up. I had resigned myself to just sitting here until I couldn't stand to do so any longer. What if he planned to keep me hostage in here all night? The thought alone was too much to bear. I was a lot more resilient than I thought I could be. It was obvious that Dean must have told the cleaning crew to skip his office tonight; otherwise, they would have been in here by now. There were times that students, and professors pulled all-night sessions in this building, so it wouldn't look odd if I left in the wee hours of the morning, if he ever decided to return. By 11:00 P.M., I tried calling again, hoping that the time gave Dean a moment to calm down, but he still didn't answer. I lay down on the cold tile floor in the fetal position. I was trying to use my own body heat to stay warm. The cold tiles against my naked skin were bone chilling. It matched what happened in this office earlier. After about another hour I dozed off.

~∞~

"Get up," he said sternly and forcefully.

I could hear his voice, but was too afraid to respond. Too afraid to even look at him. I knew no matter what I did or tried to say it would not go over well. I remained silent.

"I said get ya ass up," he repeated.

"Please, Dean, I don't want to fight you." I was trying to appeal to his rationale.

"You think I give a damn about what you want?"

"I didn't mean it like that, Dean."

He inched closer to me and I immediately braced myself by covering my head.

"How could you disrespect me like this, Zee? I trusted you. I poured everything I had in me to give into this relationship and you just didn't seem to care enough to be enough for just me."

There was finally some semblance of compassion in his voice.

I had a moment of clarity and thought about what he just said. Here I was, beaten choked, dragged and broken down by this man, and he was asking about my respect toward him. He managed to be the victim and I was the villain in his eyes, but I didn't dare mouth those thoughts, I just remained quiet.

"Oh, so now you don't have anything to say? Earlier you wanted to explain yourself, so go ahead, explain yourself."

"I know whatever I say isn't going to satisfy you, it won't be what you want to hear."

"Try me."

"I am so sorry. I don't know how else to tell you how much I am dying inside because of what I did." I couldn't bring myself to tell him the truth, even if it would help salvage whatever we may have had left. I just couldn't tell him that I had absolutely no recollection of talking with Quincy about my job, or inviting him to visit me, agreeing to go out afterward, or saying anything to him that would give him the impression that it was okay to kiss me. I just couldn't say all of that, because by doing so, I would have to tell him about my condition, about my memory loss, about my depression and anxiety. I would have to tell him that there may have been a possibility that I had seen Quincy on more than one occasion, or had even been intimate with him. There was no win-win here, if I told him the truth, he would know that I lied to him at the beginning of our relationship, and if I didn't tell him the truth, he would have to assume that I just wanted to cheat on him in our workplace to try to hurt him. Either way, I lost. This is usually where my relationships end, and the pain begins. My significant other at the time just thinks I am crazy, and they leave, so I wouldn't be surprised if Dean left as well.

"Is it because I shared with you my condition? Is that it? You were trying to find a way out?"

"I guess," I lied, knowing full well that had nothing to do with it.

"Zee, in the beginning of this, I sincerely asked you to give us a fair shot, to just try to see if we could build something, and the first chance you get, you are trying to get with someone else."

I could hear the pain in his voice. It was as if my assumed betrayal of his trust was too much to bear. He sounded so disappointed in me and my actions. It was as if he would never recover. It sounded like a familiar pain he had experienced time and time again in his lifetime.

"I know, I know. I'm so sorry, baby, I promise, if you just let me make it up to you, if you just give me another chance, I can make it right, I can fix it. I mean besides the kiss, nothing happened."

"Nah, I'm good. I'm tired of giving chances to people. Here are your clothes."

I got up, and reached for his arm. "Dean, wait," I pleaded.

"Don't touch me, Zee," he said through clinched teeth.

I could tell he meant every word, and I didn't want to press my luck.

I tried to get dressed as quickly as I could. I could feel his eyes on me. On every inch, as if he knew that it would be the last time we would be able to hold each other. After I put on my shoes, I grabbed my purse and headed out the door. I didn't even look back. I didn't want to be reminded of what could have been. I always ended up here, full of regret and questions. Full of hopes and dreams deferred.

It was a brisk night, and the lights in the parking lot seemed extremely bright. My heels clicking on the newly paved lot seemed deafening. I sat in my car and couldn't even bring myself to drive off. I tried to rationalize his behavior, in my mind, he must've wanted to give us a chance, why else would he take my clothes, he knew that would keep me in his office. If he really wanted me out, he could have just done so immediately. After about twenty minutes, I saw Dean walking across the parking lot to his reserved spot. He looked defeated, as if the whole world was on his shoulders. I knew he regretted the day he met me. I stared at him, hoping he could feel my eyes watching, begging him to turn around and acknowledge my presence but he didn't. He got in his car and left.

Back at home, I was glad I could finally get into bed. I took some of my anxiety medicine and washed it down with three glasses of wine. It was extreme for me but, I was trying to forget about this day, this life, this existence. What if I could never get myself together enough to be in a committed relationship? Everyone always leaves. Even I leave sometimes and float into another world, one where I can hear the voices of women who are or were instrumental in my life talking to me. Their voices ride so smoothly over the crashing waves that float in my mind. One of those voices would say, "It is better to light a candle than to curse the dark," and I was in a dark place right now. I wanted to see the good in the situation, but was having a hard time doing so. I wanted to light a candle and illuminate the madness I was feeling. I wanted to think of a solution.

The weekend was here, perhaps I could pick myself up together enough to face the world again on Monday, and after I took the home pregnancy test that confirmed my suspicion, I had no other choice but to try.

Saturday came and went with no fireworks. I stayed in bed all day, and drowned my tears and sorrow with more pills and more wine. I tried to call Dean, but my numerous attempts went unanswered. I left several messages, begging him to at least talk to me. He would have to reckon with the situation eventually. I would tell him about the baby growing inside of me, and if I was right about the man he was, he would want to be a part of his/her life. Sunday came and I willed myself out of bed and into the shower. I decided that I couldn't have a repeat of yesterday. I had to get out of the house and be in the company of someone who wanted me. At the end of the day, everyone desires that feeling of being wanted. I was no different. I decided to call Quincy, since there was obviously no hope for me and Dean any longer, I figured I might as well go for it. I couldn't afford to be alone with my own thoughts. I could be dangerous, and it wouldn't end well.

He answered on the second ring. Thank God.

"Hello, Mr. Buroughs. Can I cash in that raincheck?" I said playfully.

"Are you sure you are going to remember that request this time?" He laughed.

"Oh, I'm sure," I replied.

We made plans to meet at his gallery and order some lunch. While there, I had an opportunity to see some pieces that I missed the first time around. We sat in the gallery and talked about some ideas I had about attracting new customers and making his place of business the new "go-to" spot for professionals and millennials alike.

"You know I was thinking, perhaps you can partner with some local schools and have the art teachers choose some pieces that they could explore with their students. I could help write the curriculum. You could have different themes throughout the school year that highlight certain pieces. The visit from different schools could garner a lot of attention. If teachers and staff like it, I can almost guarantee they will be back on their own leisure and time. I'm also a part of a book club, maybe we can plan a session here, or even better yet, every time we finish a book we have a dinner party, would you be open to letting us host it here?"

"Wow, Zee, you are amazing."

"What? Whatever." I blushed.

"No, Zee, I mean it. You are full of such great ideas, you have a great personality, and you are so easy to talk to," he said.

"Okay, keep going, keep going, I won't complain!"

We both laughed.

"I really like the idea, but my one condition is you are here to make it come true. I know how to recognize and buy great art pieces, I don't know how to make sure this place stays full of people who admire and buy the art." I want people to look at art like I do, to see the intricate lines, the blending of colors, to feel the artists' story, to fall in love with it.

"I think I could help with that." I still have a full-time job, but with us getting ready to go on winter break, I could perhaps help out in here for a few weeks, and you know, set some preliminary things up."

"I would really love and appreciate that. What would be the first event? I know you have already thought of one."

"Well, I think the school partnership idea is a more long-term project, one that will require an action plan and a small team to develop, but for starters how about a re- grand opening event?" I suggested.

"You mean just a grand opening?" he said, almost embarrassed.

"Wait, you mean to tell me, you never even had a grand opening? No wonder people don't know about this place! You are lucky you are in such a great location. We were lucky to find it ourselves."

"Speaking of which, what is going on with you and the gentleman who you were in here with? You two a thing?"

"A thing? What are we, in grammar school?'

"Ha, ha, very funny. You know what I mean, are you seeing him exclusively?"

"No, I mean at least not right now."

"Well, from what I remember of our first phone conversation, he wasn't doing a great job making you feel wanted. I am not sure why you feel you need to put up with that."

"Oh, so you are an expert on making women feel good, huh?"

"Not really, but I wouldn't mind making you feel good."

He made his way toward where I was and we embraced and kissed like I've never kissed before. I mean kissing Dean always made me feel like wanting more, it was salacious, full of lust, but this kiss was more sensual, more involved, like he was trying to tell me that I was worth more than I gave myself credit for. It could be all the alcohol I drank yesterday, or that my mind was still reeling from what happened with Dean, but as God is my witness, Mr. Quincy Burroughs could have gotten it right there in the art gallery. He was a gentleman though, he stopped and we continued our conversation.

And that is how it remained between me and Quincy. Our relationship was rooted in conversations. Really good conversations. I mean this man had an opinion about everything, and of course so did I! We debated about the true legacy of Barack Obama. He insisted that the love affair that black people have with him is rooted purely in emotions. He wanted me to actually cite how Barack was any different, policy wise, from any other president. He said the things that mattered most, around housing, drug policy and foreign policy remained the same or even worse under Barack Obama. Of course, I countered with the powerful image that the POTUS and his wife portrayed for an entire generation. How distinguished and thoughtful he was, and how he did try to address issues, that no one before him even attempted like US-Cuba relations, or race problems. In addition, having a darker-skinned black woman by his side solidified that he would have our vote pretty much bar none. We discussed criminal justice reform, the image of the black woman, education, poverty, and everything else under the sun. We made sure to speak to one another either in person or over the phone at least once a day, sometimes even more than once a day. We sometimes talked until the wee hours of the night. He would often use the excuse of planning the grand opening as the reason for his call, but I didn't mind, I enjoyed his company. I was so grateful that winter break gave me a chance to distance myself from Dean. I even told Quincy about my pregnancy. He wasn't thrilled, but he proved to be a great support. He didn't hesitate to let me know that too much time had already passed without me telling Dean. He often gave me a man's perspective on relationship issues. I was grateful for his honesty and transparency. I was less than two months pregnant, when I finally mustered enough courage to let Dean know.

I called him on his home phone, hoping he wouldn't just hang up on me.

$\mathcal{D}$ e a n

I couldn't believe this woman! I knew I was taking a risk, but she didn't waste any time betraying my trust.

Just like that, she just threw it away. If I didn't have to see her for the rest of my life it would be too soon. She had the nerve to say that besides the kiss, nothing happened. Like that would make it better. The damage had already been done. I was even kicking myself for thinking for a nanosecond to give her a chance. I should have known the night she came to my house unannounced, her ass was trouble. There were plenty of signs. People show you who they are fairly quickly, we just have to choose to believe them. I hadn't seen her all day, and I knew she would be anxious about returning to work, so I took special care to check on her and make sure she was all good. I told her to meet me after teaching her last class, but decided I would just meet her instead, at her classroom and show her how much I missed her. Well, I was in for quite a show. There she was, with this art dude's lips all on her neck and lips. She stood rigid, with her arms to her side, but that didn't negate the fact that she let this dude touch her in that way. All of this after insisting the day they met, that he didn't try to get with her. For him to be bold enough to come to her job told me that she may have been plotting this all along.

I told her that I didn't take getting into relationships lightly, they were a big deal for me. I told her that I demand a lot from the woman in my life, and she told me she was willing to try. Honesty is key for me. That is where I draw the line. I might have even been willing

took great pride in what she had accomplished during her time at the school. I was willing to bet that she would rather sit in that office, and wait for my return than to expose what just transpired. Had I not done so, she may have acted off of sheer emotion and left the office putting both our careers at risk. Only time would tell whether or not she would air this dirty laundry.

I couldn't spend too much time worrying about it. It has always been my philosophy to not spend too much energy on things that I didn't have control over. This is mainly the reason why I like to control everything. I hated not being able to call the shots. Consequently, I try to control anything and anyone that is in my life. I know that a lot of it stems from my past. When I was a child I couldn't control the fact that my uncle would use me as a human punching bag. Whatever he was upset about, he took it out on me. If he had a bad day, if he lost too much money on drugs, if he didn't have enough money for drugs, if I left a dirty sock on the floor, his beatings didn't have any rhyme or reason. It was almost like his beating me was therapy for him. My aunt was just sick. I could only guess that she was sexually abused as a child. I read that once you are, you are more likely to sexually abuse others. I don't know if that is true or a myth, but I know what happened to me. No child should have to experience sexual acts with an adult. She would use me to satisfy her needs and each time I would throw up afterward. Going to a military boarding school for high school saved my life. It allowed me to have order, discipline and build a brotherhood with classmates. Some of whom I still keep in contact with today.

After I left my aunt's and uncle's house, I vowed to never again let anyone have so much control over me. Later on in life when I was diagnosed with residual schizophrenia, I knew that I had to be extra careful about who I got close to. I took my relationships seriously, too seriously at times. This scared most prospects away. The women who did attempt to stay could not function under the pressure I put them under. I wanted and needed order. I only colored within the lines. If they wanted to venture off and live beyond my carefully placed parameters, there would be hell to pay. That didn't necessarily mean me putting my hands on them, but it did mean yelling, screaming, blaming and shaming them into submission. When I learned how to better manage my condition, and sought therapy for my past, things got better. I was still cautious however, about the women I dated. It made me so mad that after thinking Zee might be partner, friend, and lover in my life for the long haul it ended so abruptly. I must admit, I didn't see this one coming. I thought we shared a connection. Our lovemaking was legendary. I loved being between her legs, holding her, kissing her, and I loved the way she made me feel. She knew how to meet my needs both sexually and emotionally. Her body was warm, her spirt had a calming effect on me, so much so that here I was trying to immortalize her, forgetting that she was just like all the rest: a selfish, self-centered liar. The more I tried to convince myself to vilify her name, and curse the day I met her, I couldn't do it for long. Truth was, Zee was amazing. She was someone who I really wanted to build with.

The phone was ringing. I could see it was Zee, even though I had told her countless times not to call me. After a few moments, she gave up calling my cell phone and was now calling my house phone.

"Hello, Dean?" She sounded exasperated.

"What do you want? I thought I told you not to call me," I said firmly. I didn't want anything to do with her, and I wasn't budging.

"I know, but we really need to talk," she responded.

"Zee, I don't want to talk to you, this has got to stop." I was trying desperately not to go off on her. Truth be told, I still had some choice words for her and given the opportunity, I would not hesitate to go all in.

"Dean, please, just listen," she pleaded.

Long pause. I could tell she had the words right there dangling on the tip of her tongue, but they wouldn't come out. It annoyed the shit out of me.

"Come on, Zee! Damn it!" I shouted.

"Dean, I'm pregnant."

Those words hit me like a semi-truck. Everything around me seemed to stand still.

"What! What the fuck? Pregnant? Are you serious?" was all I could manage to say, in that order. It precisely captured what I was feeling.

"So that is what I wanted to tell you," she said softly.

In an instant, my rage turned into concern and I missed hearing her voice.

"Wait, Zee, damn, where are you? I didn't mean to yell at you. I need to see you," I said.

"I'm at home right now, but I have a few errands to run. I can meet you later tonight if that works for you."

I was hoping my conversation with Zee that night in my office would be my last. I was hoping I could just move on and pretend that whatever we shared was over, that it was some type of fantasy I conjured up in my head. But with the news she just shared, that was going to be impossible now. If in fact she was pregnant with my child, it would mean that we would be forever linked. We would be connected to one another despite the animosity and mistrust. We would be responsible for bringing another human being into this world.

Here comes the pain again.

Chapter 6

I'd Rather Be Alone

Zee

I didn't have any errands to run. I just needed some time to get my thoughts together. It had been at least a week since I had last seen Dean. I knew if I had let him, he would have come over immediately and I wasn't ready to see him face to face. I called Quincy and asked him to come over and help me through what I was feeling. He was busy preparing some lunch for us both, when he accidently cut his finger.

"Oh, my goodness! Are you okay?" I asked.

"I'm fine, it was just a small cut, I just need to clean it and cover it up, you have any Band-Aids?"

"Yes, check the master bathroom, the cabinet over the mirror."

When Quincy came back from the room, I was up, trying to put the finishing touches on the delicious Kale salad he was making. I could feel him standing near the dining table, but he had yet to say anything.

"You find what you needed?" I asked.

"Yeah, I got the Band-Aid, but I also got these."

I froze. I knew before even turning around what he was talking about. My mind was racing trying to figure out what I was going to say.

"Zee."

I finally turned around. "What are you doing going through my stuff?" I asked defensively. I attempted to make this about him rummaging around my cabinet, instead of the issue at hand.

"Going through your stuff? Zee, I was looking for a Band-Aid, remember?" He looked at me like I had six eyes. He was not impressed by my ignorance.

"Oh, and then you just happened to help yourself to a tour of the entire cabinet," I countered.

"We are not going to turn this around on me, Zee. This is about you, I'm your friend, what is this about?"

He held up my prescription bottles of Latunva, and maprotiline, my anti-depression and anxiety medication.

"Zee, please don't stand there and try to think of a lie, I have friends who suffer from depression. It's okay to talk about it."

Every word he uttered was laced with sincere concern, but I couldn't afford to be blindsided by him, ever again.

"Look, sometimes I go through a rough patch, and just need a little pick-me-up, that's it and that's all. It's not a big deal, I mean I don't even remember the last time I took either one of those."

"Really, Zee? Is that what we are doing now? I am trying to be your friend here, and you are just going to act like this ain't some serious shit. What is wrong with you?"

"Well, then be my friend and believe me!"

"Zee, are you taking this medication now while pregnant? Does your doctor know?"

"Like I said, I haven't taken them in a while." My voice became louder and more egregious.

"All right, when you are ready to be honest with yourself and with me, give me a call."

He finally relented.

He grabbed his jacket and made his way toward the door. I wanted to stop him. He was by far the closest thing I had to a true friend. He had been nothing but kind to me, and yet in still, I couldn't let go of my pride. Why couldn't I just come to grips that people suffer from mental illness? This concept was hard for me to grasp. I handled it by seeking therapy when needed, and taking my medication. I didn't want anyone to know. I had a persona to uphold. I was a strong black woman. I wish Quincy could see how hard it was to tell anyone, especially a man, that I had these issues. These issues that had plagued me for most of my adult life.

I finished making the salad and then just did some light chores while I waited for Dean to come over. I knew my stomach would be in knots when I saw him. Despite how he treated me, I just couldn't shake him.

If given the choice, I would still try to make it work with Dean, and I made no apologies for it. I knew, however, that was a long shot.

When he finally came over, he just kept staring at my stomach.

"Are you going to say anything, or are you just going to look at me all night?"

"Don't get smart," he said.

"Look, I know this isn't what we planned, but we're here now."

"How do I know you didn't plan it? You may have been plotting this all along, I mean how do I even know this child is mine? The way your ass let niggas just kiss all over you, this could be someone else's baby."

It was a low blow. It hurt like hell, but I knew he needed to say it. He was still hurt and was still looking for a way to hurt me. Hurt people, hurt people. I knew this all too well.

"The baby is yours, Dean. I wasn't sleeping with anyone else, while I was with you."

"How did I end up being a part of a fucking cliché? I'm a need you to take a test, or whatever you got a do, because it's hard for me to believe anything you say. Truth be told, I really don't even know who you are for real."

"I make one mistake, and you want to crucify me. I'm sorry, Dean, I know…."

"Stop, I didn't come over here for this, I just wanted to make sure you were good. If this baby is mine, I want to make sure you're good, so do you need anything? Have you found a doctor you trust yet? I know some pretty good doctors in the area. What type of insurance do you have? What about your diet, are there some foods you should stay away from, or some that you need to have an abundance of? Are you taking any prenatal vitamins?

He rambled on and on with his pre conceived notions and ideas of what he believed expecting women needed.

I must say I was impressed, but not surprised. This man was as responsible as they come. I was still worried though. With his diagnosed conditioned, and mine, I was starting to think that I was setting this baby up for failure. I wasn't sure if mental illness was genetic but if it was, this baby would already be starting off with the odds stacked against him/her. This wasn't even counting the fact that he/she is African-American. Doubt was creeping in heavy, and I was second guessing even having the child.

"I am not even sure if I want to have the baby, Dean."

There, I said it. If honesty is what he wanted, that is exactly what he would get.

"What the fuck? What would make you say some crazy shit like that? If that is how you were feeling all along, then why would you tell me about the pregnancy in the first place? Did you think you were going to get my approval? What type of games are you playing? You are not going to have blood on my hands. Besides, if this baby is mine, that is not a decision you can make on your own."

"It's my body," I said, without blinking.

"That's fucked up, Zee. What the fuck is wrong with you?" His anger was building slowly like a pot of covered boiling water, just about to reach its boiling point.

"Will everybody stop saying that! There is nothing wrong with me, okay!" I yelled.

Before I could blink, Dean was standing so close to me I could feel his breath on my face.

"I thought I told you don't you fucking raise your voice at me."

"I know, I just—"

"You just nothing, I swear to God, Zee, next time, I gonna give you something to yell about."

"So is that what I have to look forward to? You beating my ass when I get out of line? That is the type of relationship you want to bring a baby into."

"Relationship? Who said anything about a relationship? You're fucking crazy, you know that? I don't even know why I even came over here. Just contact me when you are ready to give me the details about taking the paternity test, I don't have time for this bullshit."

The finality of his words was like the closing curtain of my favorite Broadway play. All the characters had taken their final bow, and the house lights were coming on amidst the thunderous applause of the audience.

We were both part of the story, but it was like he couldn't even stand to be in the same room with me. I needed the curtains to reopen. I wish I could start this whole drama filled production of ours again from Act I. I promise it would be different. I would take the time to learn my lines this time, I would know to exit stage left when the time came, I would hit my mark and speak confidently. Instead, I remained frozen in time, like a school girl with stage fright. I drew a blank and couldn't draw from the fountain of strength easily accessible to everyone else around me.

"Don't leave, please, don't leave," I begged.

"I'm sorry. I have just been so stressed lately, I feel like the walls are closing in on me. Can we just try this again? Please?"

"Try what again exactly, Zee?" His tone was sarcastic, and a bit insulting. "When you say can we just try this again, do you mean the part where you say you are willing to abort the life growing inside of you? Or, that I essentially don't have a say on whether you do or not? Or perhaps it's the fact that you cheated? Exactly what part of try again were you referring to?" he said matter-of-factly.

I could tell he was trying to get a rise out of me. He wanted me to meet him on the road of rage and be just as condescending as he was being. On any other day, maybe I would have been driving a semi-truck down that same road, but not today. Today I needed him. I needed him to see me, to understand my trepidation, my fears, my perspective. His lenses were only allowing him to see his side, and that was unfair.

"Dean, I just want us to move forward and work together and try to figure things out… together," I said sincerely.

"Dean, I just want us to move forward," he said, mocking me and my attempt to reconcile this whole situation.

"You really think your half-baked, half-ass apology changes anything? I am not here to try to move forward with you, I am here to accept my responsibilities, but you won't even let me do that. You know why, because somewhere in that twisted head of yours, it's still all about you right? I guess as long as you are straight, the world can continue to spin on its axis!" he exclaimed.

The lid on the boiling pot had just toppled over. His voice was filled with fury and passion, laced with displeasure and mistrust.

The room seemed light for the time of day. The remnants of the earlier sunset were just settling down like a fine dew on my windowpane. My curtains were drawn and the contrast between the beauty outside and the darkness inside was telling. My preoccupation with his resentment and my dejection was eating away at my core. I could feel the pain and the love for this man down deep. His stoic stare cut through me like a knife. It had the power to touch my soul. His eyes burned into me, as if he was trying to complete an unfinished sentence. The sound of the radio in the background slowly playing John Coltrane's "After the Crescent" seemed like the perfect soundtrack to our broken scene. My heart kept the rhythm of the song. It was the perfectly timed piano that accented this master-piece long enough to notice that his eyes were the sax-ophone playing what seemed to others erratically, but in perfect unison with all the other instruments. This was truly a Love Supreme.

"I don't think you know what you want to tell you the truth," he finally said after we both let the moment subdue us enough to reemerge unscathed.

In a way he was right. I didn't. My head was spinning and I was trying to gain control, to hold on to a fraction of what I was feeling. I wanted to be able to just lay it all at his feet, and hope he could handle it. I wanted to share a defining moment ear-lier with Quincy too, who seemed eager to really help me, but it had taken me years to even get to a point where I could share half of my feelings with my therapist, Dr. Fritz. I didn't need two more people in my life psychoanalyzing my every move. I just wanted to be normal.

I often wondered what it would feel like to live in a world where you weren't constantly in battle with your mind, with your own thoughts. In a world where you didn't have to second guess everything you did, where you didn't cling to people to somehow illuminate your light, but your light shone brightly on its own. It shone based on your own merit. I wanted to live in a world where you recognized the face staring back at you every day. Sometimes I do recognize me, but oftentimes I don't. That is the part that I wanted to share with Dean, with Quincy, with my best girlfriends. The lost-and-found part. The two worlds, the coping to function part. How do you take that step without causing a full on collision? My mind raced all the time. ALL THE TIME, but I didn't know what it was chasing. They wouldn't know how it feels to just be stuck, to be trapped by your thoughts day in and day out. I wanted to be free, but was too afraid of what freedom entailed. I was too afraid of the answers I would discover when my silence was broken.

"First you tell me you're pregnant as if you are keeping this baby, then I come over, and you are telling me you are considering terminating the pregnancy. Which is it?"

His words hung in the air, and brought me back to reality.

Therein lay my life story. The inability to choose, but more importantly the inability to recognize that I even had a choice.

"I don't know. I am just worried about what this means. It isn't like we can get a re-do. Once we have this child, it's forever. I'm just saying I may not be ready for that. I don't even know if you are truly ready for that, but sometimes I feel like I am. Like I could be a good mother, that this may be exactly what I need. It's hard to explain."

"Zee, please don't pretend to know what I am, or am not ready for. Having a child doesn't change anyone. You are who you are, if anything, having a child just exposes it."

"I disagree," I said.

"I don't care." His voice, like a door slamming shut. There is no perfect time to have a child. There will always be reasons to not have one.

"Can you give me one reason to have one?" It was my plea. I had already opened up to him, but I don't think he even noticed. This was the best attempt in my lifetime, to offer a bit of my genuine self to him, and I needed him to read between my lines.

"I don't know what you want me to say, Zee." His voice softened just enough to encourage me to go on.

"Tell me you love me," I said.

He paused for a moment as if the request caught him off guard. I could see him thinking very carefully about his response.

"I care for you, Zee. I don't trust you right now, but that will pass. It may take some time, but eventually…"

He ended the sentence but it was incomplete, it was like a dangling participle. It was a lie. I knew he would never be able to trust me.

"Will it pass? I feel like everything I do or say is always going to be questioned or scrutinized by you."

"I am not here to discuss our relationship, Zee. You keep trying to navigate the conversation back to you and me. There is no you and me, not together in that way, at least. I have to be 100-percent clear with you. I am here to talk about our plans for this child. I want to let you know that this baby will be loved and cared for."

"But what about me?" I pleaded.

"Shit, Zee! Have you been listening to anything I have said? You are like an unrelenting mad woman, bent on getting your way. What about you?" he said cynically. "The fact that I am here shows that I care for you."

I could tell he was trying to keep his composure. He wanted to remain level-headed, and prove that we could find common ground.

"You can care for a dog, you can care for your home, I need more," I said.

It wasn't coming out right, I couldn't get the words to fit on the same page he was on. I sounded desperate.

He stared at my Winnie Mandela framed poster above my sofa. His eyes avoided looking at me this time. After a long pause, he continued.

"All right, I'm done. I can see that this is only going to go around in circles. I need to go."

"I'm not trying to make you want to leave."

"I can't tell. You have done nothing but sound like a conniving, spoiled, entitled ass, since I got here."

He couldn't hold back any longer. I knew it was coming. All of his effort to try to remain calm vanished, and I had finally hit a nerve. It wasn't my intention to make my living room a hostile war zone, but here we were being contemptuous, and mean toward one another. The battle lines had been drawn, and I was waving the white flag. I was still in love with him. I was infuriated with myself for loving this man. I still saw us instead of seeing me.

"I just wanted to let you know some of what I was feeling."

"So you're feeling like you should abort our child, without any input from me, you're saying that I basically need to commit to us, in order for you to move forward. Stop me when I start misinterpreting your words."

He threw another grenade onto the battlefield.

"I didn't want our seeing each other to be adversarial," I said, my voice cracking. I didn't want to cry. I know that showing that type of emotion only leads to trouble, but my tears were like an extension of my pain. My heart ached for what I hoped to find with him, through him and by his side.

"I'm not the enemy, Zee," he said, like it was his last bullet in the chamber. He was no longer going to engage in this conversation.

He was still making his way to the door, and I couldn't stomach to watch another man walk out on me today, so I just headed to my room, my chest heaving up and down and my head staring at each step I took. I got into the shower and let the hot water run down my body. I have always liked hot showers. I like to set the water on "barely tolerable." The type that makes you think when it first hits your skin that there is no way your body could handle this type of heat, but you train your mind to stand there and endure it, until it feels like a second skin and you are willing to turn the temperature up just a little once again. Those very hot showers were therapeutic for me. They relived my pain, and eased my mind as much as any session with Dr. Fritz could. As my body adjusted to the water temperature, I admired the thick cloud of steam it created. The faux fog was dense, and served as a natural humidifier. It gave me a moment to reflect, or to try to not think at all. I was still reeling from how inept I was in my conversation with Dean. I was kicking myself because I felt like I had the chance to say exactly what I needed to say to Dean, but couldn't find the right words. I rambled and sounded bitter and vindictive, when in fact I wanted to be vulnerable and honest. I looked up and Dean stood at the shower door naked. He slid open the glass door without saying a word, and just like that, my hope was renewed. I knew I was reading too much into it. I knew in my head that he was here because we both had needs. He stood behind me and let the water run down my body as he placed his hands around my waist and joined the water by placing wet kisses on my neck. This man knew all my spots. He massaged my breast and held me so tight. I could live in that embrace forever, His broad shoulders, his chiseled stomach, his frame, his beautiful body was one that should be on my wall alongside the other masterpieces of work. His strength was everything I needed right then and there. I felt like he had enough strength for the both of us. He kissed and massaged my head with such care and, held my locks so gently. He let his fingers methodically trace my shoulders, my thighs, and my back. He took his time, and treated my body like an intricate puzzle. I loved being in this moment with him. This was the Dean that I wish I could be wrapped in forever. He turned me around slowly to face him and grabbed the soap and have done that for so long, I probably didn't know any other way to live. My body language, on the other hand, was spewing off self-doubt, concern, but love at the same time. I am certain he knew that my feelings for him were beyond measure, and he only needed to say the word for me to be back in his life. My body language was telling him that I needed him in mine.

We lay spooning for a little while, before I got up and grabbed my phone, I set it on the portable speaker and looked for my R&B classics playlist: Track 12:

> There's a light that cannot shine
> Until you come into my life
> And love reveals you will be the one
> The one for me
>
> And I'll give you all I have to give
> All the love
> All the joy
> My heart can give
> Hoping you will share the same with me
>
> (Come share my love)
> Won't you come share with me?
> Pretty baby
> Come into my life
> Share my love

Music always seemed to be our common denominator. Ever since our first outing, we connected over music. His collection of various artists only rivaled mine. We both liked different genres as well, as long as it spoke to our soul, that was all we needed.

"What you know about Mikki Howard?" he teased, half smiling. Those pearly whites, and succulent lips were like an added bonus for talking with him.

"Ah, you don't want none of this playlist," I said dramatically, like a promotor during a prize fight. "She is one of the most underrated artists of our generation…and this…this is one of my favorite songs."

"True. So is that how you feel?"

I thought about it for a moment. "Um…more like the 'Baby be Mine' track."

"Really?" he asked, with sarcasm laced in his voice.

"Yes. Really," I repeated.

"I guess we will just have to see how things go, Zee." His voice was draped in seriousness that suddenly set the light mood we were sharing back to heavy.

I walked back over to the bed, and laid my head on his chest. "Dean, I am so sorry, I want you to know that I would never set out to intentionally hurt you."

"Zee," he interrupted after a heavy sigh.

"Wait, let me finish, please," I said. "I still want you in my life, is what I am trying to say, it's all I have been trying to say all night."

"Things are a lot more complicated now, Zee. You can't do what you did and just think we can pick up where we left off, when things were going well. I told you from the jump that trust and honesty were important to me." This time he didn't sound angry, but not ready to forgive.

"Baby, what about tonight, isn't that like picking up where we left off? We are so in tune with each other," I said, my ear was pressed so closely to his chest that I could hear his very heartbeat, and I was hoping that his answer would be my lifeline as I drowned in this ocean of hopelessness.

"Like I said earlier, Zee, I am ready to be here for the baby. I can't commit to anything else right now, and I won't lie to you just so you can hear something that will make you feel better about us."

"So what was this then? I am just to believe that this was nothing?" I said calmly.

"No, it was definitely something, it just wasn't everything you want it to be. We both have needs, and we chose to fulfill them. That's it and that's all."

His brute honesty was killing me softly.

"Everything is so damn cut and dry with you all the time. Are you devoid of any feelings? 'That's it and that's all,'" I said, mocking him. "That's not all," I protested, "at least not for me."

He grew silent, brooding, as if he wanted to say more, but didn't want to upset me even further than he already had. I knew that took a lot for him, he was not one to bite his tongue. I think he knew how vulnerable I was at the moment. Exposed. I was bearing my heart to him, and he still wasn't ready to say what I needed to hear.

"Why don't you want this baby, Zee? What's the real reason?"

"I'm scared."

"Of what?"

"Of everything. Of me, of you and your condition, of how we will coparent. I mean half the time you act like you can't even stomach the sight of me, and the other half you are making love to me like it's going out of style."

"What part of YOU are you afraid of?"

"I'm not sure the type of mother I will be. I can be so aloof, at times, like, I don't know if I have that mother gene, those motherly instincts, those things don't come naturally for me."

"Everything you are saying is normal, Zee. I would imagine all new mothers may feel the same way and I don't think it is a reason to not want the baby. If you think about it, it isn't like we were really trying not to get pregnant. I wasn't using protection, and you were okay with that."

"I know."

"So, you knew there was always a risk."

I was silent. He was silent. He was also right. I didn't put anything in place to prevent this from happening, so maybe somehow I wanted it to happen. I was just so confused, I had a million questions, and feelings of self-doubt were invading and overtaking my very being. Depression is multi-faceted. It was attacking me in this moment, and I wish I knew how to make it stop, or at least slow it down.

"Do you think you can whip up some breakfast for a brother?"

He must have sensed that the room was becoming too dense, as if the steam from the shower the night before had suddenly reappeared.

Despite everything, this man made my heart smile. "Of course, I can," I said smiling from ear to ear.

I took my phone and found my old school hip-hop playlist and as "Paper Thin" by Mc Lyte, "If I Ruled the World" by Nas, and "It Takes Two" by Rob Base and EZ Rock's voices and melodic rhythms blasted through my home, I got busy making some grits, veggie omelets and vegan sausage patties.

We ate and talked some more over breakfast. As I stared at him sitting across from me at the table, I was starting to feel like maybe, just maybe, we can pull this thing called parenthood off.

"How are you feeling? Any morning sickness?" he asked.

"Um, just a little. Nothing too serious."

My phone rang, before he could ask another question, and after looking at the number I chose to ignore it. This was not the time or place to try to reconcile with Quincy. I had to remind myself that he was the one that walked out on me.

"So you not gonna answer your phone?"

"Nope."

"Why?" he probed.

"I don't feel like it, and before you jump to conclusions, it's not because you are here. I just don't feel like talking to anyone right now."

"Who's calling you, Zee?"

"Nobody."

"Okay. Look, I gotta go, I will check on you a little later," he said abruptly, cutting his breakfast meal short.

"Wait, so because I won't tell you who's calling me, you are ready to just get up and leave?"

"No, I am leaving, because you just don't get it. Lies come out of your mouth like water. You lie for no reason, that's what you do. I asked you a simple question, and you can't come correct. If that nigga calling you, just say so."

"What does it matter who's calling me?" I said defensively. "Less than thirty minutes ago, you basically said that we were a non-factor, remember? Mr. That's It and That's All, you don't get to have it both ways, act like you don't want a relationship, but then ask questions, and make accusations like we are in one."

"Later, Zee."

"Good, be out. Bye, I'd rather be alone."

Chapter 7

Make Him Do Right
Zee

The walls were closing in on me. I couldn't breathe. I was hyperventilating, and needed air, but I couldn't move. I slid down the wall I was leaning against. I figure if I got close to the ground, I could gain some ground. I have been here before, many times. This reoccurring nightmare was nothing new. I have been suffering from anxiety attacks and depression for the past ten years. The room was spinning and my chest hurt. I was beginning to cry because the medication didn't matter, it helped to mask the pain, but it didn't get to the root of the pain and I didn't know what could. The pain was excruciating, but it wasn't necessarily physical pain, it was mental. I felt like each time I was in this familiar place, a piece of my mind slipped away and I was trying my hardest to hold on. The room was now spinning faster. I used my feet to try to stomp myself back into reality. My repeated stomping on the floor was my way of trying to snap out of it. I closed my eyes and imagined myself at an open window about to jump. I did, and began free falling in the air. I tried to stop and open my eyes, but I couldn't. It was like someone was physically holding my eyes shut, holding me down, so that I couldn't move. My lips were covered, and each time I tried to move I was helplessly stuck. I use to have episodes like this when I was younger. My grandmother used to call it "the witch riding my back." That was the only way she could describe it. It was sheer terror for me, the feeling of wanting to escape and come back to existence, but not being able to, literally feeling like the strength of 10 men were preventing me from opening my eyes, or being able to speak or move any part of my body. I had long since given up on making these scenes go away, I had only hoped I could manage and conceal it enough so that it never happened in the company of others. I always took extra precaution when having male friends, lovers or girlfriends sleep over. I would take more than my prescribed dosage of medication and wine right before going to bed and would hope that the concoction would knock me out enough to not have to deal with any misfortunes, and with that and a prayer, things seemed to always work out, and on the rare occasion that it didn't, I just blamed my temporary lapse of mindfulness to too much alcohol the night before.

I remained in this state of paralysis for what seemed like forever, but was probably more like ten minutes.

Once I came to, I sobbed, drank some water and just rocked back and forth with my knees close to my chest. The repetitiveness and rhythm helped to calm me down. It was soothing. This was not the life I wanted for myself or for anyone else. It took me at least twenty minutes to convince myself not to just take the whole bottle of pills and go to sleep for good. I felt like I was just counting down my days, knowing full well that it was just a matter of time, when the thoughts that I feared, and at times welcomed the most, would consume me and take over, and I would finally go over the edge. Quincy was right, I needed to share this information with my doctor, but more importantly it was becoming crystal clear that bringing a life into this world would be devastating to say the least.

I walked out of the clinic feeling relieved and troubled. I felt guilt, but it did not override the relief. I was feeling guiltier of the competing feelings more than anything else. I would have to come to terms with my decision. It was a decision that I robbed Dean of sharing. If he thought I betrayed him before, he would surely think I was the devil incarnate now. I had no other choice. I would not bring myself to go through with it. I was selfish, but more importantly, I was sick. I knew how sick I was, but refused to come to terms with the fact that I could have, should have or would have. What's done is done. I felt cold, heartless and in charge. I wanted to be in control of something, and if that meant, my body was now a tomb for two souls, then, I would have to deal with that as it come. I don't even remember fully making the decision. I don't know when I confirmed it in my head. One moment, I am having an anxiety attack, and in the deep depths of my depression, and the next minute I am riding the metro to a discreet looking office building that was non-descript from the street. One in which, people pass every day, but may not know the stories that enter and exit the building on a daily basis. The woman who took me in the back room was kind, non-judgmental. I don't remember much of what she said, but I remember being told that I shouldn't go home on my own, that someone should pick me up. I lied and said I had a ride that would be meeting me later. It was quick. I remember the gown I wore and the cold table with the long sheet of white paper. I didn't cry like the first time. I lay perfectly still and let them do their job. I thought about my rights and the rights of those who oppose my decision. Those who stand on the front lines, protesting my right to choose, my right to make decisions for my life. How dare they? They fought for the life growing inside me, but wouldn't fight for my wellbeing? They stopped fighting for the baby once it was born, after that you were on your own. They didn't care about my mental health, or my ability to possibly harm myself or the child, that type of thinking didn't serve their agendas. They merely thought they were being a voice for the voiceless.

I looked down at my wrist, and noticed they were bruised. Why was that? I must have blacked out during my episode the other day. I wondered what other parts of my body would be unrecognizable to me. Some days I would get up and not even recognize the reflection staring back at me. I didn't want today to be one of those days. I was dreading making it back to my apartment. I was compiling a list of books I could read to help me escape this reality. I thought of some of the CDs I could listen to nonstop, perhaps dozens of times in a row, without anyone interrupting me. I settled on Karyn's White's 2nd LP, "Sandra Cisneros' Women Hollering Creek," and a bottle of white wine. My books and music may change, but the wine was constant.

I sat in the same position, wallowing in self-pity, when the phone rang. I looked at the caller ID and didn't hesitate to pick up. It was my mother. I had her listed in my phone as "Warrior." That is what she is to me. She would never know the true depths of my pain, but as a mother she was my biggest critic and also my biggest fan.

"Hi, baby." Her subtle Haitian accent greeted and soothed my mental heartache at the same time.

"How do you always know the perfect time to call? I was just thinking about you," I said.

"Mother's intuition, I guess. What is going on with you, my darling? I haven't spoken to you in a while, you okay?"

"Yes, Mummy." I still laugh that I pronounce it that way when talking to her. Growing up in a household where one parent/both try to assimilate to the language of America, I often traveled and navigated both worlds. I would say "Mummy" instead of "Mommy." I didn't even know that the term headscarf was called so until well into my teenage years. I just always called it a "mu-tra." Which is the Creole term for it. I thought every family member drank "Kremase" (a Haitian-type spiced milkshake) and enjoyed butternut squash soup on New Year's Eve or ate rice with dinner every single day. I live and embrace the rich tapestry that is my culture now, but it wasn't always that way.

"Tell me what's wrong, baby."

"Just trying to deal with another episode, Ma."

"Have you been taking your medication?" she asked. Concern laced in her inquiry.

"Yes," I lied.

"What's his name?"

That's my mummy. Always on point. "Dean," I reluctantly answered. "Dean Foster."

There was no use lying to her. She could probably see right thru me over the phone.

"Hmmm, he sounds like trouble," she responded.

"He is."

"Krik," she said.

"Krak," I responded in anticipation.

The Haitian way of starting a story. The call and response. This was my way of knowing that she was about to weave something together that would try to resonate with my pain, my struggle, my existence and I hoped I could grasp the meaning.

"Di M' ki sa ou renmen, m'a di ou ki moun ou ye," is the familiar Haitian proverb she began with, which means: "Tell me what you love and I'll tell you who you are."

"You know when I was pregnant with you, your father didn't want me to have you. He insisted that I have an abortion. Once he realized that I was not going to, he stopped talking to me for about seven months. Even though he didn't talk to me, or acknowledge my presence, I didn't leave. I still got up every morning and made him breakfast. I made sure he had his lunch and dinner every night when he came home from work. I cleaned and made sure his laundry was done and his clothes were ironed and folded every week. I didn't miss a beat. Back in my day, you didn't leave. You made it work. But what I also realized was I was not going to allow his actions or inactions to define me or determine my steps. I loved that man. I loved him with all I had. I loved him hard. I made the decision to stay. There was even a time, where he saw me downtown walking, and drove right by me. He didn't stop to pick me up. Some may say I was a fool, and maybe I was. But that was my choice. Loving him revealed who I was, and I had to come to grips with that. After you were born, you would have thought I was the Queen of Sheba the way he treated me. He never said the words 'I'm sorry' but his actions from that day forward spoke louder than any apology would. I don't know what came over him or what prompted the change of heart, perhaps it was my stubbornness, my loyalty or commitment to him. I wanted for nothing. I lived in a fine house, I had all the material things that a woman would want, but most importantly, I had his respect, and his love. If you decide to stay with a man that doesn't treat you the way you imagine, understand that you have a choice. You always have a choice to be the person that is reflective of who you choose to be with. You have got to make him do right, baby, or you have to leave. If you do decide to stay, my darling, remember the axe forgets what the tree remembers."

I didn't know if I totally agreed with my mom, but that was her advice. I could take it or leave it. She never pushed her will on me, she just offered her version of advice and wisdom, and encouraged me to take it from there.

I didn't know if any man could be made to do anything. I always figured that it was either inherent, or it wasn't. I didn't think I yielded such power over what a man's actions were toward me, but maybe I did. Women are more powerful than we give ourselves credit for. If we have the power to make a man pursue us, to change his whole life in order to be with us, then why would we not have the power to make a man do right? Maybe my mother was on to something.

I smiled through the phone. "Thanks, Mummy, I will work on it," I said, fully confident and willing to at least give it a try.

We talked a little while longer. We talked about my siblings and their on-going drama. We all had some. We ended the call with our regular "I love you" and I vowed not to have her wait so long to hear my voice.

Talking to my mother always helped, but it didn't heal. I don't think anything could. I was finally able to physically get up from the floor. For the last couple of hours, I was unwilling, no, unable to physically move. I walked around my home, touching furniture and staring out the windows like it was my first time. I felt like a visitor. I was looking at some of my belongings and wondering when and why I purchased them. I constantly felt like I was living in two different bodies. One was this wonderfully confident black woman, with goals, ambition and drive, completely focused on becoming a better version of myself each day. The other body that occupied my being was one in a constant state of confusion. A woman with conflicting thoughts, with voices that I heard off and on. Sometimes, despite how irrational, I would converse with those voices as if they are sitting right there with me. This made me live in the margins of my life. I felt like I could never fully be present on the college ruled paper. I wanted to cross over the red line and become part of my own story. I felt like the corrections the professor places on your paper with a red pen, highlighting all of your mistakes. I was always on the outside, or on top of what was already written. There was always a red pen, correcting me, wanting me to spell check or start a new paragraph, and avoid being a run on sentence, but I didn't know how. I. Didn't. Know How. I took three pills, or maybe it was five, and drowned them down with some watermelon moscato. I had run out of the white wine so I didn't have to worry about figuring it out. At least for the time being.

$\mathcal{D}\,e\,a\,n$

I can't believe Zee. She was a thorn in my side, but I couldn't shake her. I knew that I should have left when I first attempted to, but I could not bring myself to walk out of the door. She seemed incapable of pulling herself together. I took advantage of her vulnerability in order to satisfy my own selfish needs. I wanted her so badly. Making love to her was amazing. I needed her touch, her smell, I needed her longing for me, begging for me to be with her. She boosted my ego, made me feel like a king when I made love to her. It was like her body was made just for me. I knew she wouldn't resist. I knew I was everything she wanted. She was right, I was doing a good job of reminding her that we were not a thing, but I was also questioning her and demanding answers like she owed that to me. The truth was, she didn't owe me anything. I hated that she wanted me to fulfill promises that I never made. I admit, I did ask her to give us a fair chance, but in my opinion, she blew that. She was the one that made my distrust for her take center stage in our relationship, not the other way around.

I couldn't help but feeling like there were some other layers to her that I hadn't had the chance to peel back. I knew she was hiding things from me. I knew that she wasn't being completely honest about who she really was, but I figure that it would come with time. I chalked up her inability to open up to me to my condition. I know now that there was something more. I couldn't invest any more time to this. I had to move on. Moving on was what I did best. I learned how to move on all my life. It was the way I became detached from

She answered after the first ring. Almost as if she was sitting by the phone waiting for me.

"Zee." It was all I managed to say. I needed to get my shit together. I would not allow this woman to turn me into a love sick puppy.

"Dean. I was hoping I would hear from you," she said, as if she didn't know me.

"Oh, yeah?" I said. I wasn't convinced. "That's funny because I tried calling you earlier this week, but I guess you weren't ready to talk."

"I wasn't," she replied.

"You can't do that, Zee. When I call, you need to answer. I almost came by to make sure you were okay. Do you understand how selfish and inconsiderate that is? I mean, damn, do you ever think of anyone besides yourself?"

I was done trying to reason with her. She needed to know the truth.

"Please stop. I can't today. If you called to just lay me out and disrespect me…."

I didn't let her finish.

"Disrespect you?" Anger hung on every syllable. "You got a lot damn nerve, Zee. You are pregnant with my child, and you decide to ignore my calls, and somehow you manage to turn this into me disrespecting you! Next time I call you, your ass better answer."

"Well, you don't have to worry about checking on my pregnant self anymore."

"What do you mean, Zee?" I asked, still trying to wrap my head around the finality of her statement.

"I mean just what I said. I am not pregnant anymore, so you don't have to worry about checking on me."

Her voice was unrecognizable. I didn't want to believe this was the same person I met just a few short months ago.

"You selfish bitch!" I yelled. "I can't believe your ass went ahead and did it anyway."

"Well, believe it. I didn't need your permission."

"Oh, I see, your bitch ass getting real bold over the phone, you fucking crazy bitch. Who do fuck do you think you are? I told you not to make that decision without me."

I needed to chill, I was taking it too far. I was becoming the demons that raised me. I knew that I should give her a chance to say something, anything to try to justify her actions, but I couldn't. She took advantage of the brief pause and tried to speak.

"Dean, I couldn't…." was all I allowed her get out.

"You couldn't what?!" I yelled. "You couldn't be a person with some fucking compassion! You couldn't be a person who doesn't murder a life! I swear to God, you are dead to me, you understand? 'Don't fucking call me, ever, for any reason, don't try to contact me in any way, shape or form, as a matter of fact, if I see you, I will be sure to beat your ass within an inch of your fucking life."

I could hear her sobs as I hung up. Cursing her out wasn't enough. She deserved to feel the pain she was putting me through. Even with the cards life dealt me, I managed to be a fairly decent guy. I could have taken my past, and the pain of my upbringing and wreaked havoc on society. I knew I wasn't perfect, but even I had lines I didn't cross. I just couldn't get over the fact that there were thousands of women, men and families out there who would give anything to have a child. I was willing to be in my child's life, to give him or her everything I didn't have, to debunk the stereotype of the absentee black father. She robbed me of that. I felt like she didn't deserve to live. I wanted to snuff her life out for her betrayal, for her dishonesty, for her lack of thinking of anyone besides herself. Didn't she know that she wasn't the only one who had doubts? Shit, it wasn't like I grew up in an ideal situation, but at least I was willing to try. I was willing to right the wrongs of my past, by being better. My one lapse in judgment by giving Zee Warren a chance was the worst mistake of my life. It turned out my being involved with her manage to push me into an episode of my illness. I hadn't had to deal with any real issues in months. I was having a relapse, not remembering things I did throughout the her car, or collect her mail, or come home with her hands full of groceries or dry-cleaning, I wanted to kill her. How dare she go on with her life as if she hadn't just killed one, and destroyed another? To me, she was the angst of my pain. She was the reason I was constantly re-living my nightmare of a childhood, my dysfunction at work, my inability to collect my bearings. In my mind, it was women like her that refused to let me do right. I wanted to be the good guy, and she wouldn't let me.

I stood still, by the side of her house, dressed in all black. I was part of the brick and mortar siding. I had become her predator. I had parked my car two blocks away from her house and walked to her residence. Like clock-work, she exited the house at 8:34, to bring the recyclable items she had collected throughout the week to the curb. When she did, I quickly slipped into her house, like a snake slithering its way toward its prey, digging its fangs into the helpless victim. I immediately made my way to her bedroom, and stood behind her door. This is what she turned me into, a mad man, one who had lost all sense of reality. In a way, I felt like I was becoming her. She came back into the house. I heard her lock the door, and finish washing the dishes in the sink. I knew she wasn't going to remain there for long. If I knew her as well as I think I did, she would make herself a snack, and then make her way to the bedroom to watch her favorite Mon-day night show, before showering and calling it a night.

well have been screaming in the middle of a forest. I swung her across the room with such force, she hit the floor with a powerful thud. I immediately used my foot to kick her in her side multiple times as she tried crawling away from me. She was a caged animal. There was no place for her to run. I kneeled beside where she was laying, helpless and defeated. I took her head and banged it on the floor before pulling out my gun.

"Open your mouth!" I demanded.

I could tell she was trying to get her bearings together, trying to come back to life in this nightmare that she was experiencing. It was a nightmare for me too. It was her fault for putting us both there.

"Open your fucking mouth!" I said again slowly and more sinister, this time I used the gun to pistol whip her into submission.

"I don't remember why I did it," she managed to say, even though her tongue was heavy and her lips swollen beyond recognition with blood dripping onto the hardwood floors.

I placed the gun in her mouth. She closed her eyes, and placed her hands on top of mine, oddly enough she wasn't pushing my hand away. She seemed to be at peace, almost like she wanted me to go ahead and put her out of her misery.

I pulled the trigger.
Click.

Chapter 8

Simple Pleasures
Zee

I woke up in the hospital with machines and IVs hooked to my arm. I managed to open my eyes to survey the room. Wrapped in a hospital blanket lying awkwardly on the long window seat, and looking extremely uncomfortable was Quincy. I was embarrassed, I had treated him so wrong, he didn't deserve that, and I didn't deserve him. I didn't deserve his friendship or for him to care about my wellbeing.

"Hey, you," I said, hoping he wasn't already in a deep sleep.

He opened his eyes and looked right at me, almost as if he was looking at me for the first time.

"Hey, beautiful," he replied.

His response was everything I needed to hear, because I knew if I was in this hospital, I was anything but beautiful.

I learned later that I had a broken nose, and jaw, and two fractured ribs. I could tell by looking in the mirror that my face was battered and bruised, and my right eye was swollen shut. I had lost quite a bit of blood. I remember the account I gave the police officer, when asked, I said I was robbed during a home invasion and could not identify the suspect. Why was I protecting the bastard? Why wouldn't I let him suffer the consequences for what he had done to me? Deep down, however, I knew why. I felt like I deserved it. I had pushed him to do this and this was the karma I received for taking a life. A life that didn't only belong to me. I was merely the carrier. This life had chosen me and Dean as vessels, and instead of embracing that notion, I disregarded that gift and threw it away. I was convinced that the pain he inflicted on me paled in comparison to the pain, guilt and shame I had put on myself.

Quincy got up and walked over to the bed. He pulled up a chair, sat close to me and held my hand. The gesture was so gentile, so loving and I knew it was genuine.

"Quincy, I am so sorry for not being honest with you," I struggled to say.

It still hurt to speak. My lips were so swollen, my tongue felt like a brick and every bone in my body ached with each word I uttered, but I had to let him know how I felt.

"Ssshh, don't overexert yourself," he said. "You don't need to do this right now, Zee."

"No, I do. I have to. I just wanted to say thank you for always being a good friend to me. I know you must hate me." Those familiar tears had appeared again.

"If I hated you, I would not be here," he reassured me.

"How did they find me?" I could only remember bits and pieces of that night. It was like a movie trailer, only playing the most suspenseful parts.

"You called me after he left and I came over, your front door was unlocked, I found you in the bedroom, barely hanging on. I immediately called the police and paramedics."

"Please don't judge me, Quincy." I felt the need to share that with him.

"I'm not, it's just I have never understood how women let men do this type of thing to them and then turn around and not press charges. This man damn near killed you."

His frustration was evident. I knew I would have to tread lightly with my logic and reasoning.

"You have got to know, I never wanted to be treated this way." I needed him to know that I didn't go into my relationship with Dean looking to be a victim.

"Then why not let him have to own up to what he did to you? Why not call the police and tell them the truth?"

It was all so black and white for him. He saw the problem and saw the most plausible answer. It was not that easy for me. I didn't want to have to contribute to the modern day lynching of another black man. Society had done that enough.

"It is not entirely his fault," I began to say.

"Don't do that, Zee. Don't you dare try to make excuses for that bastard and what he did. There is not a reason in the world for any man to justify doing what was done to you."

"I can think of some reasons," I countered.

"Look, you are not going to win this debate. I don't care what you did to that man, he could have found a better way to handle it. You have got to know that you didn't deserve any of this."

I didn't want my first conversation with Quincy, since the last time I saw him, to be an argument. He had been kind enough to answer my call when I needed him most, even though we hadn't spoken in weeks, and he was the one here with me now, so I let it go.

"Okay," I said.

"The doctors say you might be able to go home in a few days. I want you to come stay with me for a while."

"Why are you being so nice to me?" I said. Part of me wanted to believe that it was just in his nature to be so kind, but the other part of me held doubts. There was no way in the world there were genuine good guys out there, not looking for anything in return. In the recesses of my mind, I wondered what I would be forced to do to repay his gesture.

"I am being a friend, Zee. I think we can all use some every now and again."

I couldn't argue there. I made Quincy promise that he wouldn't tell my mother or anyone else about my ordeal. The last thing I needed was for this fiery island woman to head on down to D.C. to take care of business. If Dean thought I was a handful, he hadn't seen anything like the whirlwind my mother could be. I knew in my heart that if I told my mother or my siblings what Dean did to me; they would kill him. I am not speaking figuratively; they would actually kill him. I would then have to live the rest of my life with the guilt of my mother or sibling in prison for the rest of their lives because of my poor decisions. I couldn't fathom the thought, so I pleaded with Quincy to not let anyone in my family find out. It wouldn't be all that difficult, since none of my family lived near me, and only visited during holidays He reluctantly agreed.

After all the tests, counseling, x-rays and recanting my false story to the officers for what seemed like the millionth time, I was finally able to leave the hospital. I was told that my broken nose would heal naturally within two to three weeks. I could manage the pain at home with medication and that the swelling and bruising would subside within a week. My jaw would take a bit longer. Fortunately, it wasn't broken in multiple places. I had to have my jaw wired shut, but it did not completely eliminate my ability to talk. I could mumble my words somewhat coherently. I would have to be on a liquid diet for about four to six weeks. I would have the wire removed in about three weeks. The bruising and swelling of my face would fade after a while and my rib fractures would take about four weeks to heal. The x-rays revealed quite a bit of bruising of my ribs and nearby muscles and my breathing would be a bit shallow for the next few weeks. I had to monitor my movements and be careful not to perform any duties that may damage the injury even more. The good news was there was no significant, long-term damage done to my lungs. I was given a boatload of prescriptions to help to deal with the physical pain. The mixture of those medications with alcohol, which is what I often did, was a deadly combination. Quincy must have known that wouldn't be a good thing for me. I think that was the main reason why he wanted me to stay with him. He knew that having all of that medication at my disposal, with my state of mind was not a good idea. He was truly a God send. My own personal angel on earth.

I thought about how often I took the ability to open my mouth as wide as I could, or being able to eat solid food, or breathe normally for granted. I thought about my face and how abnormal or hideous I looked with all the bruising and swelling. I thought about my body aching and how I would give anything right now to be pain free.

I thanked all the doctors and nurses as I got in my wheelchair to leave. Quincy, as promised, was right there every step of the way. When I got to his house, I could tell he had painstakingly rearranged furniture, and set everything up so that I would be comfortable. The guest bedroom had all the amenities of a five-star hotel room. He had the bed made up with his expensive 800-count sheets and a beautiful comforter. He had magazines and novels on a table next to the bed. Towels and washcloths and a basket of body oils were placed on the bed as well.

"Okay, Martha Stewart, I see you," I teased.

"Ha, very funny. I just wanted to make sure you were good."

"I definitely will be. This is too much, I don't need all of this extra stuff."

"Just accept kindness, Zee. Not everyone is out to hurt you."

"Okay, okay, I will try my best. I am just so grateful. Thank you so much."

"Will you stop thanking me? The shit is making me uncomfortable!" He laughed and it made me laugh, which in turn made my sides hurt.

"Stop, don't make me laugh," I said.

Talking made my chest hurt, but I wanted Quincy to know that his acts of kindness and friendship toward me meant the world. I didn't think there would ever be a way or a situation that I could repay him.

After settling in, and putting the few clothes and toiletries I brought with me away, I joined Quincy in the living room. He had his dinner, baked chicken, mixed vegetables and potatoes looking scrumptious. I must admit, he was looking mighty fine as well. I pushed those thoughts out of my head. I couldn't afford to get infatuated with this man. I put him in the friend zone and that is where he had to stay. Besides, my decrepit and injured body wouldn't be able to do anything anyway! I laughed when I saw he took my liquid drink concoction that I would have for dinner and tried to dress it up with an umbrella and a lemon on the side.

"Ha, ha, very funny. I would rather have some of what you got going on over there."

"No, ma'am," he pulled his plate close to him. "Doctor's orders, remember? You are on a liquid diet for the next couple of weeks."

"That is so not fair!" I whined, barely audible.

"You can hardly open your mouth, how the hell are you gonna chew food!" he teased.

"Don't rub it in, I can at least smell."

"Can you?" he said sarcastically, referring to my broken nose.

I continued to help him with his gallery from home. I set up all his appointments, wrote emails and thank you notes to potential clients. I sent him in the direction of the latest artists, and gave him what he needed in order for him to make informed decisions when purchasing art pieces for his gallery. I must admit, I was pretty good at being his personal assistant. He had such a passion for the work. We would spend hours at night just going over pieces he admired. He taught me so much about artist I thought I knew, and those that I had never even heard of. In the past, I limited the art I liked to those pieces that made sense to me. The others just seemed like a two-year-old went ballistic with a can of paint. I could never understand why someone would pay thousands or even millions of dollars for what looked like a blob of paint. Quincy helped me to look deeper, and to really appreciate what those images represented. When you knew the history of the artist, when you knew their story it all seemed to make more sense. You became connected in a way that was indescribable. My favorites, however, were the photographs. The black-and-white pictures of happiness and despair melted my heart. They told so many stories of the lives of those whom I never met, but felt I knew for a lifetime. The one who really captured my heart was Jean-Michel Basquiat. At first looking at his primitive style of art reminded me of the stick figures I use to draw in class, but then I

studied who he was as a person. His graffiti art res-
onated with me, because of course I am a true hip-hop
fan. His multi-cultural background gave him a unique
lens. He had a Haitian father and a Puerto-Rican
mother, he was self-taught, and was the youngest to
have his work featured in the Kestner Gallery in
Hanover, Germany. He wasn't a starving artist for very
long. Some of his work sold for as much as $50,000.00.
He was actually an artist, making a living off of being
an artist, even though he dropped out of high school
his senior year. Despite his popularity, his relationship
with his father was strained and he had other demons
that drove him to drugs. He died of an overdose at
twenty-seven years old, just a few years older than I was.
I connected with his story, which allowed me to connect
with his work. I was one of his paintings. I imagined
myself there on the canvas. I knew what he dealt with.
I wished I had the artistic talent to put my feelings on
paper or even in a song, but it was my quiet hell, and at
times it wasn't even quiet.

I had been working all day, trying to convince a
local artist I met through social media to have his work
featured in Quincy's gallery. Some of the up and coming artists are very serious about "keeping it real," they
felt as if having a showcase was in some way not being
true to their roots. Some were perfectly fine with re-
maining underground. They weren't in it for the noto-

riety and money. But with my new appreciation for art, I was determined to discover the next Basquait, and this D.C. native, Rashawn Tridoe, was well on his way to something big. I was finally able to book him and couldn't wait to tell Quincy all about it. He came home looking so good. I felt like June Cleaver, a doting housewife, keeping all the affairs of the home in order until hubby, came home from work. It had been a while since I felt the warm soothing touch of a man. Staying at his house had me thinking all kinds of things. Each time, I repressed those thoughts and feelings. I knew trying to get with him now would not be a good idea. What had me even more worried was the fact that I was still thinking about Dean. I didn't understand why I was wired that way. Dean was the man who had caused me the most pain, both emotionally and physically, and yet, here I was, thinking about him, lusting for him, wanting to see him. I shared everything I was thinking with Quincy, but I knew better than to share those thoughts with him. He would probably render me useless, and a lost cause and kick me out of the house. It would be such a slap in his face. He couldn't stand the mere mention of the man's name. He told me once during our late-night conversations that he felt I compromised his morals, by not allowing him to contact the police on my behalf. He said however, that would be the one and only time he would stand idly by and knowingly be complicit in another man's crime. I have never forgiven myself for making him feel that way and promised to make it up to him the best way I could. I would not tell him about my feelings for Dean. I couldn't do that to him. At least, I didn't think I could.

"Hello…earth to Zee." His words snapped me back to reality.

"Oh, my goodness, Quincy, I didn't even hear you come in," I said.

"Obviously. What has got you so intrigued?" he said peering over my shoulder to look at my computer screen.

I told him all about Rashawn Tiridoe, and showed him some of his work he had posted on social media. He was impressed. He leaned down to give me a hug, careful not to squeeze too hard around my waist. Wrapping my arms around him was like a natural aphrodisiac.

"I like it; his work could pull in a whole new generation of young folks that will appreciate the arts. It could be an entirely new consumer base for us. Tell me more."

I went on to explain that Tridoe's works, his paintings and photography alike, was a collection of pieces entitled: "We Wear the Mask." It took a closer look at how African-Americans exist in the double consciousness. How we operate and talk one way when at work or with other races, and use a totally different dialect and body language when we are among our peers. How our mannerisms and way of maneuvering physically change in order to survive in spaces where we are not the majority. This is an age old adage. This work was first coined and elaborated on by W.E.B. Dubois extensively, and examined further through Phillipp Wamba's memorable work: *Kinship*. In it, he explores the struggles and devastation he felt trying to navigate through being a native African, and growing up partly in the states. It showed how double consciousness could still exist outside the traditional parameters. I think every professional African-American person I know walks this tight rope every day of their lives. I hear myself all the time, when I call to make appointments or arrangements on Quincy's behalf, or on behalf of the gallery switch up my speech depending on who I am talking to. My tone and pitch change to have the observer; the listener be at ease, to try to make myself less of a threat. My thoughts and vision are distorted because of other people's negative image of my race. I can only imagine what it is like for my male counterparts, who by their mere existence, are seen as a fully loaded weapon. Tridoe's work captured that spirit magnificently.

"I see you have been busy." He grinned with approval.

I was glad Quincy was pleased with my analysis and my research. I was excited to start planning Rashawn

Tridoe's art exhibit. I was thinking I can pair it with a jazz or conscious hip-hop open mic, or play the stark differences between what we have coined conscious rap and mainstream rap music. This would align perfectly with Tridoe's work. The ideas were running wild in my head. I knew Quincy could see the wheels turning.

"All right, don't get carried away. Niggas like Tridoe are known to flake out when the date looms closer; nevertheless, your hard work deserves to be rewarded."

"I agree."

"How about some ice cream?"

"Really? Ice cream? I feel like a kid who just showed his daddy a good report card."

"Okay, so you tell me, Kanye West, with your wired jaw, what else you wanna eat? You want me to whip up one of my delicious smoothies."

"No, no, ice cream it is. I could use something sweet."

We were so corny together, but I liked it. We were like the perfect couple on the outside, like the ones you see out in public and swear that the chemistry can't be real. It must fake. That is how we were. He held my hand as we took our ice cream and sat on the park bench near the shop. His arm lay gently around me as we talked about how dope the next event at the gallery would be. We were enjoying people watching when I felt compelled to explain.

"You know, I wanted him to kill me."

He straightened up. He just looked at me, but I kept staring straight ahead.

"I wanted him to pull the trigger. I felt like I didn't deserve to live. The physical pain doesn't even begin to match the pain I feel on the inside."

"Did you tell him about your depression?"

"No."

"Shit, Zee, that wasn't right, but it still doesn't give anybody the right to play judge, jury and executioner."

"He trusted me with so much, and I just destroyed it. I singlehandedly made it implode."

"I am no expert, but what I do know, is you have an illness, and blaming yourself about this isn't going to do anything to help you get better and maintain your wellbeing. Your condition is manageable; you just have to stay on top of your self-care."

"How do you know so much about it?' I asked. It was like he was speaking from personal experience.

"I always suspected that my mother suffered from depression, but she was never diagnosed. As a result, in college I pursued the social sciences. I wanted to learn everything about it. I wanted to help her to get better. I've just done a lot of reading on the subject. That's all. I wanted to let you know that things can and will get better."

With that, he leaned down and kissed me on the side of my forehead and then again softly on the lips. I welcomed the affection. It was tender and sensuous. He had my heart, and I didn't have to have sex with him for it to happen. I realized I was willing to get better as long as Quincy was by my side. At least for the time being.

Being with Quincy helped me to remember and enjoy the simple pleasures in life, like working on something with a purpose, with passion, eating ice cream, enjoying the sunrays. Those were all the things that I couldn't see clearly when I was trapped in the recesses of my mind. My relationship with Dean, if that's what I could call it, didn't help matters much at all. Managing my illness seemed to be plausible when I was with Quincy, but my days here were numbered. I couldn't live in this safe space forever. Eventually, I would have to be thrusted back into reality. Even when Quincy insisted that I could stay as long as I wanted, or needed, I knew that was just him being Quincy. The man had rearranged his whole life for me, I knew that wouldn't last forever. On top of all of that, I was afraid of hurting him, of doing something so despicable that he would turn on me like Dean had. I knew I was capable of doing just that. I would cherish these weeks spent with Quincy, because I needed these memories. I needed simple. I needed pleasure.

On our way back home, Quincy stopped by the gallery to pick up some paperwork he needed me to review. I elected to wait in the car. While nodding my head to the melodic beat of Bag Lady by Badu, my phone buzzed. I looked down, and there it was. Life interrupted. Dean.

...Bag lady, you gon' hurt your back, carryin' all them bags like that, I guess nobody ever told you, all you must hold on to is you, is you, is you...so pack light.

He wouldn't let me do simple. He wouldn't let me do pleasure. He wouldn't let me hold on to me.

Chapter 9

I'm Your Woman
Dean

I hated her. I hated that she robbed me of a life that I had created. It wasn't her choice to make alone, even though she was carrying the child. To me, it was like murder. I know I had not given her the best reasons to feel secure, I may have even made her feel unwanted, but I was very clear from the moment she told me she was pregnant, that I was willing to be a father to my child. How could she? It drove me up a wall to think that anyone could be so thoughtless. I know that in my life I had made many mistakes, but I felt like raising and caring for a child the right way would help me to atone for many of my sins. I knew I couldn't go back and change the horrible things that were done to me, but I could assure that my legacy wouldn't be one of failure, of misery and despair. I felt like I was finally ready to start a new cycle of hope in my own family history, and just like that it was done.

I wanted her to die. That is how much I hated her for what she did. I felt like she did it on purpose. I felt like she did to spite me, to make sure that she sent me over the edge. As much as I wanted her dead, I wanted her with me. The thought of her being with someone else made me sick. She was mine. Her body, her thoughts, her decisions, they were all mine. I did not share. I alone determined whether she could move on without me, not her. I could have killed her, and I most certainly tried to do just that. Her life rested in my hands. That night I had plenty of guns to choose from. I was an avid collector. I use to go to the gun range to help clear my mind. I chose the revolver that I had admired as a gun enthusiast at Military boarding school, and bought at a gun show almost fifteen years ago. I thought about a passage from *The Autobiography of Malcom X*. This was when he was still Malcom Little, trying to find his way in the world. He was trying to show his burglary accomplices, shorty and a white woman he was dating at the time, Sophia, that he was not afraid to die. He held a revolver to his head and took out all the bullets except one and played Russian Roulette. They begged and pleaded for him to stop, but he was relentless. I had made up in my mind that night, that I was going to do the same, in this version however, I would not be holding the gun up to my own head, it would be to hers. I had decided in that moment in time, that I would pull the trigger, and deal with the consequences. She didn't die that night because it wasn't her time, not because I spared her life. It was pure luck. Apparently, that it where I was mentally that night, willing to throw my whole life away based on another person's decision and subsequent actions. I knew I could never let them happen again, only I should be able to control what pushes me too far, not any one thing, or any one person.

It had been nearly two months, since that near fatal encounter, and I still thought about her every single day. Over the course of the last two months, I had been promoted to vice president of the Community College where we met. Zee had put in her letter of resignation shortly after I had her groveling on my office floor, the night I caught her with Quinton Boroughs. I knew she was working for him now, at his gallery, as his personal assistant. I had a fear that once word got out that the college was seriously considering me for the role of vice president, that she would come forward with her tales of the abuse that she had suffered at my hands. She never did, and for the life of me, I couldn't understand why. I had seen many careers go down the drain, because mistakes from the past weren't buried deep enough. I thought she would use the opportunity to expose who I was at the core of my being. I was in many ways just like her, cold and calculated. She never came forward. The search committee, and panel responsible for hiring me, did some serious vetting, they even managed to find out the type of student I was at the board-

had other suitors, but she was blinded by me. I was a confident man, and didn't gloat, or toot my own horn often, but I was grateful for whatever hold I had on her.

I was always one that took pride in my appearance, but I made certain that I was impeccably dressed and groomed for my lunch date with Zee. I wanted her to see me and forget what I had put her through. I wanted to see her and do the same. The moment she walked into the bar, she took my breath away. Her form fitting dress accentuated all of her gorgeous curves. Her hips begged for my hand to rub them mercilessly. Her full breasts were peeking through the top of her dress just enough to remind me of how delectable they tasted. She had her locks swept to one side, exposing another favorite part of her body, her neck. I wanted to plant a thousand kisses on her, but I knew I had to keep my composure. She looked around for a bit, before spotting me at the bar. I waved her over, and stood up to greet her as she drew closer.

"I'm glad you came."

She smiled.

"Please sit."

She obliged, and sat on the bar stool that I had pulled out for her. I went ahead and ordered her favorite drink, an Amaretto Sour, and let her take a few sips before peppering her with the questions I had.

"Like I said, I am glad you agreed to meet me, why?"

"I don't know, I guess I wanted to see you face to face and listen to what you had to say. Congratulations, by the way, on your promotion," she added.

"Thank you. Did the college ever contact you regarding that?"

"Yes, they did," she admitted.

"Why didn't you ever tell them?"

"I don't know, I felt like I owed you."

"You don't," I reassured her.

"I think I do," she replied.

"Is that why you agreed to meet me, because you felt you owe me?"

"Partly," she admitted.

"Zee, I know that nothing I say can make up for what I did to you, I am trying to come to terms with the whole thing myself. I didn't think I was capable of doing to anyone what I put you through. I was just so consumed with anger. It turned me into someone who I didn't recognize."

"I guess I can say the same thing to you," she replied.

"I was in a dark place, Zee."

"Me too."

"How do you even find it within you to not seek vengeance?"

"Well, I learned that I can't hate or judge people, because they sin differently from me. I know a lot of people that pray every day for God to forgive them for their transgressions, no matter how many times they commit the same one, and the expectation is, that God will forgive us, and give us another chance to make it right. I am not God by any shape or form, but I do believe God is within me, that I am made in his image. Therefore, I need to forgive, not so much for your sake, but for mine."

"You are a better spirit than I could ever be."

"I just know that in order for me to move forward with my life, I had to come to terms with this, and not allow my hatred for you to consume me."

"So have you moved on with your life?"

"Somewhat, I am doing work that I love, I am healing both physically and emotionally. So I guess I am taking it day by day."

Her lips were succulent, I wanted to kiss her with everything I had. I reached for her hand, and placed my hand on top of hers. Her hand was shaking.

"I am not going to hurt you again, Zee."

She half smiled and pulled her hand away. I could tell she was trying to maintain her composure. It was like she had practiced and rehearsed this encounter a million times in her head, and she was determined to follow the script.

"I don't want you to think of a monster every time you see me."

"I am getting there, but it's going to take time."

"How much time?"

"I don't know, like I said, I am taking it one day at a time," she said.

"Does hate for me still consume you?" I asked.

"I guess I can ask you the same thing," she replied.

"Zee, I don't hate you. I am not a religious man, but I want to make this right. It means everything to me that you remained loyal. Honestly, if the shoe were on the other foot, I can't say for sure if I would have done the same thing."

"I guess I was trying to be a friend. Everyone could use one every now and again, as someone once told me," she said.

"What if I told you I wanted to try again, to try giving us another chance."

"I think we both know that wouldn't be a good idea."

"Actually, I think it's a great idea."

"Let's not do this, Dean. I needed to come here as much for my own healing, and what I suppose is your need to see me."

"I wanted to hate you forever, Zee, but I can't, no matter how hard I try. I can't stop thinking about you, wanting you, believe me, if I could, I would make this whole thing just go away. I think as much as you've tried, you can't let me go either. You want me, I know you do."

"I have to go, Dean. I said what I needed to say. I am trying to make my peace with this whole thing."

She started to make her way off the stool. But I wasn't done.

"Sit down, Zee," I demanded.

She hesitated, but she sat back down. I wasn't going to make a scene, but I needed to finish what was on my mind, there was really no guarantee that she would agree to see me again.

"Zee, I can't make what happened that night go away, but I can try to live every day making it up to you. I thought I could move on, but I can't. With all our mess, I think we can make it work."

I could tell she wasn't convinced.

"Dean, I think we both know that we bring out the absolute worst in each other. It's not healthy. I just want us both to move on, and get on with living our best lives."

"I can see you are really getting into those self-help books," I said sarcastically. I wasn't going to give her the satisfaction of rejecting me.

"See, the moment you don't get the answer you want to hear, you try to diminish my voice. But you know what? I am not falling for it this time," she said.

"This isn't reality TV, Zee. This is real life. I made a mistake. I am owning up to it, and trying to make it right."

"You can make it right by letting me go. Let me move on, and try to figure things out on my own."

"Do you still love me?" I could feel her slipping away, and it was the only card I had left to play.

"Dean, please don't make me answer that."

"It's a simple question."

"No, it's not, it's a loaded question. If I say no, I sound like a hypocrite, after saying I am trying to move on and live my best life, and if I say yes, then that leaves the impression that there may still be hope for us."

"Just answer the question, and stop with all the psycho analytical bull shit."

"I have to go, Dean, please just let me go."

"It's just that simple for you, huh? Maybe the guilt trip would work."

"Nothing in my life is simple," she replied. "I really have to go, Dean. I want you to take care of yourself, okay?" she continued.

I didn't answer. I sulked. I looked straight ahead, and didn't acknowledge her leaving. This is not the way I hoped things would end. Honestly, I wasn't sure how it would end, but I was hoping it would be with us leaving together. I knew she still loved me, weather she was willing to admit or not. I just had to think of another way to get her to realize it. I wasn't done, but I would let her go for now.

She got off the stool, waited for me to acknowledge her leaving. When she saw I wasn't, she placed her hand on my shoulder for a brief moment and left.

$\mathcal{Z}ee$

I needed to meet with Dean for me. I needed to confront my biggest fear, in order to move on with my life. I knew I would not be able to truly be free of him, until I spoke to him. I guess I got what I wanted, he tried to apologize, but it was laced with expectations. I was not willing to compromise the work that I had done on myself since the incident. I know he did not take that well. He was so unpredictable. I knew that this was probably not the last I would hear from him.

I walked into the home, I was now freely sharing with Quincy and the lights were dim. As soon as I placed my keys in the tray by the door, I saw Quincy sitting on his favorite recliner, with a drink in his hand. I couldn't make out if he looked upset, but I was in tune with his energy, and I could tell he was not happy. I thought for a moment that maybe Tridoe had called and cancelled his upcoming appearance, but I knew that would not have Quincy in such a dark mood.

He didn't waste any time revealing the true source of his contempt.

"How could you, Zee?"

I didn't want to play dumb, not with this man. He had been too good to me. I knew exactly what he was talking about. I wasn't sure how he found out, and it didn't matter. I made up my mind that my relationship with him would not be built on lies.

"I needed closure, Quincy," I said. It wasn't just a made up excuse, it was the truth.

"You needed closure from this fuck nigga. The same nigga that tried to murder you? That's who needed closure from? After everything he put you through, you agreed to meet with him?" He made it sound like I was a fool for even suggesting such a thing.

"I just wanted to close that chapter in my life. I needed to do it for me, Quincy, for us, please know it had nothing to do with our relationship. It had nothing to do with you."

"Really? So why not tell me about it?" he asked.

"Because I knew you would not approve, I didn't want you to think I was disrespecting you by seeing him, I didn't want you to be angry with me, like you are right now."

"Fuck that, you have been living with me for the past few months, we share everything, I'm the one that found your ass nearly half dead and helped you, I am the one that was there for you every step of the way during your recovery. That nigga you needed closure from didn't give a fuck, he didn't care if you lived or died, and this is how you repay me…by getting back with this nigga?"

"I am not back with anyone; it wasn't like that. I just needed to see him to finalize everything," I emotionally asserted.

By this time, I had made my way to where he was sitting and stood in front of him. I needed him to know, that my meeting Dean, had nothing to do with how grateful I was that he was by my side throughout this whole ordeal or how fortunate I felt to be developing a relationship with him.

"You could have finalized everything over the phone, as a matter of fact, I thought him trying to kill you was final enough. You don't owe this nigga nothing."

"I know. It really wasn't even about him, it's just what I thought I needed to do for me. I am sorry, Quincy, please don't…."

He didn't let me finish.

"Just get out."

"Get out?" I was confused. He couldn't be ending our friendship over this.

"Yeah, get out, get your things, I will give you until the end of the day tomorrow."

"Why are you doing this, Quincy? I...."

Again, he didn't let me finish.

"Why? Why? Because you went behind my back to meet with a nigga that don't give a shit about you, you lied to me and told me you were going to hang with your girls, because I thought I could trust you, because who's to say the next time this nigga calls and needs to see you, you won't go running on the strength of needing some god damn closure. You can save that text book bull shit for the next dude, and the fucked up part is you know how I feel about this whole situation. How I had to come to terms with aiding and abetting a fucking criminal, because of my friendship with you. You know what that means, Zee, it means that I put aside my morals, my values and what I wanted to do for someone else. You should try it some time. Bitches like you don't ever learn 'til you six feet under."

His last statement hit me like a ton of bricks. The entire time that I had known Quincy, he had never disrespected me. He never raised his voice, not even in the slightest way. He had never called me out of my name. He had been nothing but kind and endearing. He took care of me in a way that I had never experienced with another man. He was concerned about my entire being, and most importantly of all, he knew about my condition. I was so hurt. Tears were falling. I never meant to hurt him, even though I knew that eventually I would, I just didn't know how. I wanted to express to him once again that my meeting Dean, was not intended to disrespect him, but I was so caught up in my emotions, I knew my words weren't coming out right.

"Bitch?" I said. "So that's what I am now, a bitch?"

"What else would you be?"

"I'm your woman, Quincy, I don't deserve this, not from you."

"My woman?" He laughed, as if that idea was implausible. "Really, is that what you are? Naw, you could never be that, because my woman wouldn't do what you did for a motherfucker that tried to kill her."

"You're not listening, Quincy, it wasn't like that," I pleaded. I didn't want to lose him. It would be worse than what Dean had done to me.

"Oh, I am listening just fine. I hear you loud and clear. Your needs and wants come first, no matter how they may affect others, that is what I'm hearing," he said.

"I'm sorry, maybe I should have handled it better, but I didn't intend to hurt you in the process."

He became stoic.

"So the thing with me, Zee, is you don't get all the chances in the world to fuck with me, once you disrespect me, I'm done." There's no need to try to seek closure with me, because I am telling you right now I am done with you. You got hella shit you need to figure out in your life, and I can't be there to support you with that. You need to do that on your own, some of this shit can't be attributed to your depression, Zee, you have to realize what makes you a fucked-up person and deal with it. I need you out by the end of the day tomorrow," he concluded.

I resigned that my pleading and reasoning with him would not allow him to remove his pride from the situation, so I just agreed.

"Okay," I replied. I didn't even try to continue. I was defeated. His words stung like a million bees angry that their honey had been harvested, and just realized the power they possessed. I had no more fight left in me. He managed to take it all.

Chapter 10

Thinkin' 'bout Love
Zee

I sat in my home, and tried to put the pieces of me back together. I felt like a million pieces of my being were floating around the universe, not anchored to anything. With everything that happened, I knew one thing for certain, I needed to learn how to love me. I needed to learn to put myself first, and as selfish as that may sound, I was okay with it. I had to work on the part of me that manages to hurt those closest to me, the part of me that refuses to let anyone get too close. Love has to come from within, before it could be shared with others. When there is no enemy within, the enemies outside cannot hurt you. I don't know what I was going to find, but at least now, I was willing to look. I was willing to look for the person I needed when I was younger, the person I needed when I was violated, the person I needed, when I was near death. Quincy was right, I had to come to terms with what made me who I am, what motivated me to do the things I did. I didn't like facing that person in the mirror, but I had to stop running from her and avoiding her like the plague. I had to confront all parts of me, my past, my present and my future.

It had been at least a month since Quincy kicked me out of his home. I tried countless times to reconcile with him after our falling out. I was still saddened that our friendship and budding romance ended the way it did. I saw a future with him. We were taking it slow, and that was the best thing for me. He hadn't yet returned any of my calls, or responded to any of my texts or emails. The gallery sent me a letter in the mail shortly after our falling out, stating that my services were no longer needed due to budget constraints. I guess he was a man of his word. I decided that I wasn't ready to give up on the idea of us. I knew he needed time, and I was willing to give him all the time he needed to meet the woman I was becoming. The one thing about working with Quincy is I polished my skills, and learned a lot about the art industry. I sent my resume to a few places and was hired as an administrative assistant with an elite gallery downtown. The pay wasn't nearly as much as I was making as a professor, but it was enough to keep me afloat and give me piece of mind.

Dean tried reaching out to me a few times after our brief encounter at the bar, but I never answered. I didn't answer because I needed to prove to myself that I could manage without him. I didn't need him to anchor my pieces for me. I didn't want to imagine what life with him would be like. I was terrified of him and would forever fear him. I couldn't bear the touch of him without shaking and reliving the nightmare in my head, and that would be a horrible way to exist in a relationship. I still loved him, and sadly, if he persisted, I couldn't fully trust myself that I wouldn't go falling back into his arms. Our love was like the misty rain that falls softly, but floods the river. Eventually I would drown.

Although I was no longer officially working for Quincy and his gallery any longer, I still had all of the files and appointments on his calendar saved on my computer. I realized that the showcase by Tridoe was this evening. I had to be there. It was my first full project and I was determined to see how it all turned out. I had done everything to prepare for a flawless night before I was terminated. I hired the caterer, the jazz band, the hip-hop artist and arranged for a photographer to document the event. I sent out invitations to all current and former clientele, teachers, local city councilman, news outlets, art enthusiasts etc. I needed to see all of my hard work come together. I wanted to be proud of something I helped to create. I reasoned in my head that I may not even see Quincy, I could be in and out before he even noticed I was there.

I decided on a maroon form-fitting dress that stopped right above my knees. It fit nicely, not too tight, but snug enough to show off some of my curves. I pulled my locks up in a high bun and exposed my neckline. I coupled the dress with some accessories and added my beige high-heel designer shoes to complete the ensemble. I looked at myself in the mirror and was pleased. Once I arrived at the gallery, I was elated that there were quite a few people milling around outside. It created a buzz for those people just walking by and enticed them to stop in. It was like perfectly placed advertisement for the night's event. When I stepped into the gallery, I was even more impressed with the size of the crowd enjoying the night's festivities. A number of people were actively engaged in bidding for some of Tridoe's pieces during a silent auction, some were talking with one another, networking and exchanging information, while others were listening to the hip-hop artist eloquently weave words together describing the concept of wearing the mask, still others were enjoying the light hors d'oeuvres and jazz music, and several pockets of people were posing for pictures or taking selfies to add to their social media pages. I was so pleased that it had all come together. I really wanted tonight to be a success for Quincy. He deserved it more than anyone I knew. He worked hard to build a space for the community that everyone could enjoy and have it be multi-dimensional. It didn't only serve as a great place to appreciate the fine arts, but as a meeting space for artists and local activist as well. He was even thinking about expanding and adding a full service restaurant. I knew that the sky was the limit when it came to his ideas. After a few moments, I spotted Tridoe, talking to potential customers. I walked over to him, re-introduced myself and struck up a conversation. He was intriguing. He was kind and grateful that I had reached out to him and convinced him to take a leap of faith. His work was selling and he couldn't be happier. When Tridoe walked away, I remained standing there alone and indecisive. I didn't know which corner of the vast room I should head to next. Truth be told, I really had no reason to stay any longer. My mission had been accomplished. I was able to see the turnout and talk with Tridoe, and yet I remained frozen. It made me feel small in a room full of people. I was appreciating the jazz music when I heard the voice.

"You are a vision, a sight for sore eyes."

I didn't have to turn around to know it was Quincy. I knew his sultry voice like the back of my hand. My nerves were getting the best of me. I was almost afraid to respond, to turn around and face him. This is why I didn't leave. He was who I was waiting for.

"Hi," was all I managed to say, but I remained facing forward, pretending to gawk at a rather large art piece on the wall. I wasn't ready to look at him. A flood of emotions were overtaking my body. I suddenly felt lightheaded.

"I was hoping you would come tonight," he said, further cementing my utter confusion at the moment.

"Really? I didn't think you wanted to see me." I figured there was no need to be vague.

"I know how hard you worked to make tonight possible, you deserve to be here to witness the fruits of your labor."

He was standing so close behind me I could feel his breath on my neck. It was warm, and he smelled delectable. I wanted to fall back into his chest and have him wrap his arms around me, but I knew it wasn't the time or place for any of that. I wondered when he noticed that I had arrived. I hadn't seen him at all with all the walking I did to find Tridoe.

"I am so happy for you, Quincy." It looked like those books I passed over at the silent auction table were filling up fast. I tried to keep my composure, but I was fading fast.

"I'm happy for you too, Zee, I always knew you had it in you," he complimented.

"Can I ask you a question?" I asked.

I was desperate to know why he was being so kind to me. His last words to me were still etched in stone in my mind, and yet he was acting like we were long-lost high school buddies at a class reunion. It was sending my mind racing into a hundred different directions.

"Of course," he replied.

"Do you think we could...." I couldn't finish the sentence. It was like saying it out loud would force us to relive that night, the ending of our relationship, and I wanted nothing more than to move forward. I know he must have sensed my apprehension.

"Maybe, Zee. Maybe," he answered.

It was all the confirmation I needed. I grinned so hard that I was glad he was still standing behind me. He was so close, he could have impregnated me with both our clothes on.

"Zee, there is this exhibit called the Clothesline Project at the National Museum of Women in the Arts in Washington, D.C. You think you might be interested in checking it out with me?"

I was at a complete lost for words. I sincerely thought that he had written me off. I turned around to face him. I had to look for the truth in his eyes.

"What does this mean, Quincy?"

He paused for a moment, before answering as if he was trying to figure it all out himself.

"It means that I have heard some great things about this exhibit, and I think you would enjoy yourself. It also means that I would like very much to see you again."

I grinned slightly before answering. "Okay. I will be sure to call you and let you know when I am available." I wasn't ready to dive off the cliff just yet. That had always been my problem.

He gave me a look that could only be described as indignation, before responding. "Okay. That's fair."

He placed his hand on my hip for a moment and kissed my neck and cheek ever so gently. His kiss felt like a day of reckoning. We were forced to deal with our unpleasant past in this space, if only for an instant.

I watched intently as he walked away to greet and meet new patrons, talk with artists and mingle with the crowd. He was so elegant and imposing. He wore a light blue tailor-made suit that fit him perfectly and accentuated his well-defined frame. His brown wing tip shoes made him look even more sophisticated and his freshly shaven face and hair made his eyes shine full of life. I admired him from a far, all the while remembering that he too could be cold and calculating and mean and hurtful. He also didn't fully understand me but I concluded that I was willing to take my chances.

I stayed a little while longer appreciating all the great art pieces and the ambiance the night created. I was overjoyed that everything turned out so well. It validated that I was capable of much more than I had given myself credit for. It gave me the boost of confidence I needed to call Quincy later to confirm our date.

The next morning I sat on my balcony with some water instead of wine, and thought about love. I was still trying to figure it out. I was taking my medication regularly and had an appointment with Dr. Fritz set up for tomorrow. I held the phone in my hand for the past twenty minutes trying to muster up the courage to call Quincy. I don't know why I was so nervous; after all, he was the one that suggested this outing. I finally called him and we agreed to meet at the museum.

The Clothesline Project was created by Monica Mayer, a Mexico City based artist back in 1978. The exhibit centered around several questions: Have you ever experienced violence or harassment as a woman? As a woman, where do you feel safe? and, As a woman, how did you or how could you regain your joy after experiencing violence or harassment? The questions were answered on pink notecards and clipped by clothespin to form an array of perspectives. It helped to open many conversations similar to the Me-Too movement started by Tarana Burke. I was extremely grateful that Quincy had chosen this exhibit to visit.

As we walked along the halls of the display, he held my hand and we talked about some of the responses recorded. We noticed and discussed how the answers covered all angles. The multiple attitudes showcased that although we may have experienced the same pain, our coping methods were as different and the same as the sun and the moon.

"If given the opportunity, what would your response be to these questions? Where do you feel safe?" he asked.

No one had ever taken the time to ask me that before.

"I feel safe with you, Quincy. It's like I'm jumping on a trampoline, but I am not afraid to jump as high as I want, because of the safety net around me," I responded.

"So I'm like your security blanket." He sounded uncertain.

"Well, I guess, but not in a juvenile nonsensical kind of way," I reassured him.

"I want you to get to a point where you find that security within you, Zee."

"I know. I am trying to work on that," I said. "If you don't mind me asking, why did you decide to give us another chance?"

I had to know.

"I never stopped thinking about you, Zee. I was just hurt, confused and angry to tell you the truth. I knew you would be at the showcase, and I would have a chance to see you."

"But why not return any of my calls, or respond to any of my emails?"

"Sometimes, Zee, I cannot hear what you say for the thunder of what you are. You are like a storm, and

I had to be sure that I was ready to deal with that," he said sincerely.

Being there with Quincy showed me once again, how very thoughtful he was. In the midst of how I made him feel by seeing Dean behind his back, he still thought enough of my wellbeing to share this experience with me. This made me admit that I may have finally found my kindred spirit. Quincy made me unearth feelings buried deep within the crevices of my soul and I wanted him now more than ever. I wanted nothing more to share my existence with him and to love him beyond understanding.

I know things weren't perfect but sometimes just thinkin' bout love sets you on the right path. That's all I ever wanted, to be headed in the right direction. After all, to get lost is to learn the way.

Chapter 11

One Minute

Quincy woke me up from my slumber with a sweet kiss on the forehead. His lips were soft and wet. After last night's trip to the museum and dinner, we headed back to my place and shared such intimacy with one another. Our lovemaking was unlike anything I had ever experienced. Not even with Dean. It wasn't just physical; I could feel our bodies becoming one as we made love, as if our souls were intertwined. It was the thing that I had only seen in melodramatic movies or read about in romantic novels. He kissed and caressed every inch of my body. He acted as if he wanted to heal all my wounds. He took the time to study my body, to ask questions, to want to know what I liked and didn't like, he introduced me to parts of my intimate place that I didn't know could be aroused. He aimed to please, and he wanted to be satisfied as well. He told me exactly how to help him reach the ultimate heights of pleasure, and I did my best to not let him down. It had taken us so long to reach this point. I cried while he made love to me. It was the first time that I was with someone who knew all my faults and was still willing to try to find the solutions with me.

"I wanted to run some ideas by you about an upcoming event at the gallery," he said after the flutter of kisses on my forehead had subsided.

"Well, you know, that type of service will cost you. I no longer work for you, remember?" I said with a sarcastic smile.

"Oh, so you are going to charge me a consulting fee?"

"Yes, and I will take payments in the form of…," I said, eyeing his private part mischievously.

"Don't sell yourself short, business is business."

"Believe me, there is nothing short about you."

We both laughed as we discussed his plans as part of our morning pillow talk. Afterward we shared our plans for the day, and he was pleased to hear that I intended to see Dr. Fritz later on. He even offered to go with me, but I declined. Although Quincy was the first man I had let in on my other world, I still wasn't ready to relent everything about me to him. I needed the safe space of Dr. Fritz's office to sort out my issues. Maybe in time, he could join me, but not today.

I arrived for my appointment with Dr. Fritz and sat in his office waiting for him to come in. I always liked sitting in his office. It was warm and welcoming. Everything from the paint color on the walls, the comfortable furniture, the decorative pillows and art were all very soothing. I wondered if they learned to do that sort of thing in school, like was it part of the curriculum to create a certain type of space for clients. His desk was neatly organized, to the point that I suspected he may have OCD. Everything was in place, it looked like it could be an ad in a print catalog. Before my appointment, Dr. Fritz had emailed me and asked if it was okay for his latest intern to sit in on my session. I had obliged before, so I agreed that it would be fine. I always reasoned that just like in any profession, people need hands-on experience with little to no degree of failure to truly appreciate and master their craft before striking out on their own. He had several interns over the years, that I been a patient of his, and they were all very nice. Once the session started, however, I was feeling a bit perturbed that I had agreed to let his intern, Francine, sit in on the session. She seemed nice enough, but for some reason her look bothered me. I felt like she was trying too hard to crack the code, as if I was a science experiment. It was almost as if she was waiting on me to say something that would suddenly provide the both of them with all of the answers they needed to cure me. He left the room for what seemed like a lifetime, and I indulged myself for a bit, and unleashed a bit of what I had been dealing with lately. She gave textbook an-

"Wow," Dr. Fritz, "Zenia is amazing. I learned so much in that short amount of time. I am so glad I am getting the chance to observe you while you work with her. Thanks for letting me talk with her for a bit privately," Francine said.

"Amazing? Well, that would be one way to describe her, I guess," Dr. Fritz replied.

"I mean, she has been through so much heartache. It's incredible how she is able to compartmentalize all of her issues, and feelings."

"Well, you are right about that. She has been through quite a lot. Wait, what exactly did she share with you?"

"I mean, not much, her dating life mostly, just some details about a guy named Dean and Qu…."

"Ah, Dean and Quincy, why yes, of course. You finally got to hear about them."

"That is an intense love story."

"There is no love story. Dean Foster is the Director of this facility, and Quincy Burroughs is a volunteer that visits with his fraternity, reads to her about once a month and shares some of his freelance photography and artwork with her."

"Listen, Francine," he continued, "Ms. Zenia Warren lives in a world based on fantasy. This is a first-class, maximum-security facility for patients who suffer from extreme schizophrenia, manic depression/bipolar and psychosis. Don't ever forget that. You are here to do a job, albeit with compassion, but don't get caught up with these patients. Zenia has been here the longest. She was committed when she was nineteen, after she tried to commit suicide for the fifth time following a brutal rape she suffered during her sophomore year in college. At first, it was thought, that she was only raped by one person, but there is speculation there may have been more than one perpetrator. Based on her chart, however, she most likely was suffering from this illness well before that traumatic incident. She will tell that fabricated love story about Dean and Quincy to anyone who will listen. Half of the staff knows that story. She's pretty good at it. All she does pretty much all day is listen to Karyn Whites' CD.

Francine came back into the room with a puzzled look on her face. I wanted to ask her what was wrong. I wanted to know what she thought about what Dr. Fritz told her. Had he shared my entire chart with her? She half smiled at me. She looked nervous, like she was afraid I might say or do something to have her run out of the room. I saw her make her way over to the small table near the window. She picked up my favorite CD. Karyn White's 2nd LP, and seemed to be reading the track titles on the back. I could have told her what they were, if that was what she wanted to know.

Track 1: Hungah
Track 2: Can I Stay with You?
Track 3: Weakness
Track 4: Nobody but My Baby
Track 5: Here Comes the Pain Again
Track 6: I'd Rather Be Alone
Track 7: Make Him Do Right
Track 8: Simple Pleasures
Track 9: I'm Your Woman
Track 10: Thinkin' 'bout Love
Track 11: One Minute

I saw Francine, the intern, put the CD down and start to make her way out the door, she was moving fast, like she had just seen a ghost.

"Wait," I said.

She turned around and I saw that look. That "look" had become all too familiar. She was looking at me differently. She was judging me. She was placing me in a box that I didn't deserve to be in. She was trying to figure out where the blurred lines of my fantasy and my reality intersected. The truth was, so was I. Names, dates and places can change. The story remains the same. She thought I was crazy, like the rest of them, but I wasn't. I am a strong black woman, planting my foot into my existence. I am remembering me.

"One minute," I said.

Facebook: booktherapy19
Instagram: Book.therapy_
Website: www.booktherapy.us